Amy Maxwell

&

The Long 9 Months

Heather Balog

Amy Maxwell & the Long 9 Months
Heather Balog

This book is a work of fiction. Names, places and incidents are either a product of the author's imagination or used fictitiously. Any resemblance to actual persons, living or dead, events or locales is entirely coincidental.

Copyright 2019 Heather Balog
All rights reserved. Except as permitted under U.S. Copyright Act of 1976, no part of this publication may be reproduced, distributed, or transmitted in any form or by any means, or stored in a database or retrieval system, without the prior written permission of the publisher.

Cover design by Blurbs and Baubles

Published 2019
Published in the United States of America

Dear reader:

Amy Maxwell & the Long 9 Months is a prequel to the rest of the Amy Maxwell series. While no exact year is ever established, it takes place about 14 years before *The 8 Mistakes of Amy Maxwell.* This is the early 2000s, the beginning of the 21st century, and things were a bit different than they are now. Remember life before technology took over everything? Dial-up internet and pagers? Not having cell phones or cameras at our disposal? Ahhh....the good old days. Enjoy Amy's madness BEFORE children.

Heather ☺

P.S. If you've never met Amy Maxwell, what are you waiting for? Check out her adventures exclusively on Amazon:

~Prologue~

Oh my God! This is nuts! An insane amount of pain! I really think this kind of pain should come with some sort of warning. Did they warn me it would hurt this much in that class? Or all those books I read? I think not. And Mom didn't warn me about this either! I have a few choice words for her *when I'm done with this, that's for sure.*

I know they said it was painful, but my God! They could have mentioned I was going to feel like an antelope being torn apart by a hungry mountain lion. It's like I'm being split in half!

Okay…it's stopped for a second. Take a deep breath.

I guess Beth was right when she said I wasn't ready to be a mother. Ugh! Why didn't I listen? Well, not that there was anything I could have done about it at that point…

Why didn't I listen to the doctor and take it easy? It's too early! I'm not supposed to have this baby for another three weeks! If I had listened to the doctor this wouldn't be happening.

Wait! Is there some way to stop this kid from coming out? Or maybe someone can just cut me open and take it out? I know I said I wanted to do the whole natural labor thing and all, but I've changed my mind!

Oh wait, I have no choice. I have to do this natural labor thing no matter what! Get down on all fours, Amy, and rock. Didn't that labor coach, midwife lady tell you that would help with the pain? Do it now, before the pain starts to build again. These contractions are like a minute apart. It can't be too long now.

How did I get in this situation? Well, I know how I got into the whole being pregnant *situation, thank you very much! What I mean is, how did I get into* this *situation...giving birth...*here. *Is that a bag of dog poop over in the corner? Oh, this can't be very sanitary.*

Beth will faint dead away when I tell her about this. She would want to give birth in a pool of sea water with tinkling music playing in the background while a masseuse rubs her shoulders. Hey, that actually doesn't sound too bad right—

Here comes the pain again! Breathe, Amy! Breathe! This sucks that I have to remind myself to breathe! That should be Roger's job. Roger should be reminding me to breathe. I miss Roger! I wish he was here. I want Roger! I need Roger!

Oh my God, I'm going to scream. No, I can't scream! Bite your tongue, Amy! Or your lip. Just bite something. If you scream, he's going to know you're in here. And then *what are you going to do? How are you going to explain being in the back of a dog catcher's van, down on all fours, giving birth?*

Crap. I'm going to scream.

1

March

"Amy! Have you seen my tie?"

Roger dashes into the bedroom, face as red as a beet, sweat rolling down his neck. He is frantically attempting to pull his suit jacket on over his dress shirt, but his arm keeps getting stuck in the sleeve. It's pretty comically, actually.

I try to stifle my laughter—this is a pretty important day for him and I don't want to upset him—but he sees me smirking.

"Come on, Amy. This isn't funny!"

"You're right," I say, pointing to the ceiling fan. Somehow Roger's tie has ended up on the ceiling fan. Possibly when he was tossing clothing out of the closet yesterday, in a frantic search for dress clothes to wear for this interview.

Roger is a History teacher at the local high school and has been for the past ten years. While it's a great job, he went back to school not too long ago to get his Master's degree so he could be a principal. It was very time consuming and very expensive. *Translation:* it cost a lot of money that we really didn't have as a newly married couple. It has been over a year since he got his degree and he hasn't had a single interview. There just haven't been any openings. Until yesterday.

The principal at the school he works at flat out up and quit. He packed up all his belongings and moved to Florida. In one day. After being a principal for twenty-seven years. Apparently the stress of the job had gotten to him.

You would think something like that would deter Roger from further pursuing the career change, but no—it seems to have gotten him more fired up than ever. So now here he is, preparing for his interview this morning, gone completely berserk.

I am also getting ready for work, but my job is not nearly as stressful as Roger's. I didn't exactly excel in the world of academia and do not have a degree, so I cannot fulfill my dream of being a world-renowned journalist. I have been forced to pursue other avenues of revenue.

Translation: I dropped out of college and got married, and now I work at the pharmacy down the block stocking shelves and smiling at customers that often smell like mothballs. I don't start work until ten o'clock, so I am getting ready by reading and enjoying coffee in bed.

Well, I'm *trying* to enjoy the coffee. Not only are Roger's antics disturbing me, my stomach is feeling a little queasy at the moment. I guess I'm really nervous for him. I'd really like him to get this job. Not only would it double his salary, but I would not have to hear about how the school lacks direction and leadership anymore. He drones on and on about that *endlessly*. He was never the biggest fan of the former principal, so I think he was ready to do cartwheels across the living room when his co-worker had called him to tell him the boss had quit.

I watch Roger pace like a caged tiger as he knots his tie into his fingers. Disgusted, he toss the tie onto the bed with a grunt.

"Will you relax already? You got this in the bag. Why are you so nervous?"

"There are other people interviewing for this job, Amy. It's not a given that I'm going to get it." He picks up the tie and tries again.

"Oh please. There's nobody more qualified for this position than you are, Rog. You've been working at that school for ten years. You know what needs to be done there. They're only interviewing those other people as a formality. You know how it is in this town."

"Yeah, it's who you know. The mayor's son is interviewing for the position, too."

"Robby? My sister graduated with Robby. He's the biggest stoner on the East Coast. He can barely tie his shoes. I bet his mother has to do it for him. There's no way they'll hire that dope, regardless of who his dad is." I leave out the part that Robby was *super* hot in high school and I followed him around with my tongue hanging out, worshiping the ground he walked on. Along with every other female in the school.

"Stranger things have happened, Amy." Roger finally finishes with the tie and stomps out of the bedroom. Thirty seconds later I hear clattering in the kitchen. I don't know what he's doing, but I'm pretty sure he's going to accidentally break something—a bowl or maybe a necessary appendage.

Sighing, I toss off the covers and shove my feet into my slippers. It's the beginning of March, spring is coming in just a few short weeks, but of course it just snowed yesterday and the hardwood floors of our apartment are ice cold. I grab my lukewarm cup of coffee and shuffle down the hall into the kitchen. It's not a far shuffle—our apartment is the size of a postage stamp.

"What are you doing?" I ask Roger as I open the microwave door and place my cup on the turntable inside. Roger has two cabinets open and is looking between them with a perplexed expression on his face.

"I'm looking for cereal," he says.

"It's in the other cabinet," I tell him, pointing to the cabinet above the toaster.

"I looked there. There wasn't any cereal."

"Oh, then we're out. I'll go to the store later and get some. Do we need anything else?"

Roger gets a little flustered. "Um, no. Cereal is fine. Just get cereal." He opens the fridge. It's pretty bare. "And milk. We need milk. There's some cash in the top drawer of the desk."

I nod as I press the minute plus button to warm up my coffee and Roger glances down at his watch. "I guess I'll just grab one of these cereal bar things," he mutters as he takes a bar from the box next to the toaster. He really must be nervous. He never eats them—he says they taste like sawdust in his mouth. I'm not sure how he would know what sawdust tastes like, though. He *is* fourteen years older than me, so maybe kids growing up in the sixties did weird things like eat sawdust.

He grabs his school bag from the chair in the kitchen and looks at his watch again. "I'm gonna be late for my first class if I don't get moving."

"What time is your interview again?"

"Eleven. It's after my third class, during my prep period. I'll call you at work around noon and let you know how it went."

"Okay. Good luck." I offer him a peck on the cheek—I don't want to kiss his lips since he looks like he is about to vomit.

"Thanks," he mutters and before I can say another word, he is out the door.

I pull my coffee mug out of the microwave and head over to the desk tucked in the corner of our living room. I find it odd that Roger told me to pay for the groceries with cash. I usually use our debit card. I didn't even know he kept cash in the drawer.

I open the top desk drawer and find that there is indeed a pile of cash sitting in there, causing me to gasp. I take it out and discover that it's mostly fives and tens—about $200— not really as much money as I initially thought it was.

Next to the cash is our checkbook. Now, I don't often see the checkbook because Roger doesn't like me to touch it. Not that he's this 1950s husband who doles out money to his happy little housewife or anything. It's because when we were dating, I made the mistake of asking Roger to get my checkbook so I could write a check. He almost keeled over from a heart attack when he saw the recording register. *Apparently* you're supposed to record every single transaction to the penny or something. And you have to balance it every now and again. *And* rounding up or down is frowned upon.

Hey, I was about twenty years old at the time and no one had ever taught me anything about a checkbook. It's not like it's a class at school or anything. So when we got married, Roger took over the checkbook, which was perfectly fine with me because I hated the damn thing anyway.

I flip open our checkbook, curious to see what Roger's been doing with it this whole time and why he suddenly has cash sitting in a drawer in our house. It's my turn to nearly keel over from a heart attack when I see the balance staring back at me.

$87.94.

That's it. I don't know much about balancing the checkbook, but I'm pretty sure that means $87.94 is all the money we have in the world—aside from the $200 sitting in the drawer. We both just got paid this week and have no other money coming in until—I check the calendar on the desk—ten days from now. And if I recall correctly, our rent is due before those ten days are up.

With a shaking hand, I flip through the pages of the checkbook register, wondering if maybe Roger made a large purchase that I didn't know about and that's what caused the balance to be so low. *Or maybe he's gambling? Could he owe money to a bookie or something? No, that's not Roger. He would never gamble. He's too anal retentive for that.*

It appears that each time Roger got paid in the last year, the money was immediately sent out to pay bills. Car insurance (a tad bit high due to a fender bender I got into a few months ago), rent, utilities, and groceries. Every month, nearly every cent he made went toward a bill.

Of course then there is *my* pathetic salary. From what I can see, at the hourly wage I get, my check barely covers the cable bill.

I sink down into the desk chair, checkbook sliding out of my hand and onto the floor. I knew we weren't well off or anything crazy like that—we never eat out and we haven't gone on a vacation in ages. I don't really shop or get my nails done or anything crazy like that.

Why don't we have any money? What are we going to do? We can't live like this!

The thought of living paycheck to paycheck makes me physically nauseated. I leap from the chair and run to the bathroom. I make it to the toilet just in time to puke.

What the hell? I stare at the puke. *I really hope I haven't picked up anything at work.* Working in a pharmacy, I do come in contact with a lot of sick people who come in to pick up their prescriptions.

I stand up and wipe my mouth off with the wet washcloth I used earlier to wash my face. Sighing, I know it's time to get ready for work despite the fact I just threw up. I can't call out now that I know we really need the money. My job is not difficult and I actually really like the pharmacist, Harry, and his wife, Carol, but the hours are long sometimes, and the job can be boring.

As I walk to work (it's only a few blocks away and my car is unreliable at best—plus we never got the fender fixed after the fender bender), it's the first time that I am truly regretful of my decision to drop out of college before I got my degree. The money I make at the pharmacy will never be enough to help our situation if we are living paycheck to paycheck.

Maybe I can go back to college, get the credits I'm missing, and graduate? No, that's impossible. Enrolling for classes costs money that we don't have.

We will be stuck living in the apartment forever, barely having money to cover the rent and utilities. We'll never go on vacation. We'll never buy a house. We'll never have kids.

Unless Roger gets the principal job, I realize. I have almost completely forgotten about the interview. If Roger gets the principal job, his salary will nearly double.

My heart speeds up. *Roger's definitely going to get this job! There's nobody more qualified than he is. And they love him at the school!*

Silly me for worrying. Of course Roger had a plan all along. Roger is one hundred and twenty percent sensible. Plus, I can always ask for more hours at work. That'll give us a little padding. And in a few months maybe, just maybe, I can think about setting some of that money aside for going back to school. You know, before we have kids and everything and it will be too difficult to go back to school.

I am feeling much better by the time I get to work. In fact, I practically skip in the door.

"Morning, Carol!" I call out in a sing-song voice. Carol is the jack of all trades at the pharmacy. She stocks shelves, helps customers, answers phones. She balances the books, places the orders, and she rings up customers when we're super busy. Carol is in her sixties and she's been talking about scaling back her hours for a few months now. Carol and Harry's daughter is having another baby, and Carol wants to be able to spend time with her grandchildren and babysit for her daughter when she goes back to work.

"Hi, hon," Carol says, looking up from her accounting books. She doesn't wear her usual smile. I briefly worry that something is wrong with Harry or maybe her daughter, when Harry calls out to me.

"Hi, Harry," I say, stepping behind the counter and pulling my lab coat on over my clothes. I'm not a pharmacist or even a tech, but Harry likes us all to look sterile and professional. He says it puts the customers at ease. I personally think it freaks them out, but I can't tell Harry this. He's a nice guy, but he's definitely not as approachable as Carol.

"Amy, did you see the shipment that came in yesterday? From Pharm Lite?"

I purse my lips, concentrating. "I don't think there *was* a shipment yesterday, Harry. Wait, let me check the log." I reach underneath the counter where I keep a log of all shipments we've received—I paperclip the invoice to it until I can give it to Carol. "Nope. Nothing came yesterday at all."

Harry groans and Carol joins his side. "Oh no. You think it's those kids again?"

I frown at them. "What kids?"

Harry sighs and rubs his temple. "We think that there are a bunch of kids in the neighborhood going around stealing packages from local businesses. The business owners' association just had a meeting about this. Since this package didn't need to be signed for, the driver says he left it in front, before we opened yesterday. Carol and I come in the back, so we wouldn't have seen it until we opened to the public."

"Oh no," I groan. "I definitely don't remember seeing a package when I came in yesterday morning."

Harry shakes his head. "Yeah, that's what I was afraid of. We think that the package was stolen. There were over $3000 worth of diabetic supplies in it."

"They left a package with $3000 dollars worth of supplies without getting a signature?" I am in shock.

"Well, it's never been a problem in the past," Harry says.

"We're going to have to make sure everything gets a signature from now on," Carol tells him.

"True, true," Harry says.

"That's awful," I say, suddenly feeling an overwhelming wave of nausea, similar to the one that I had this morning. "Excuse me!" I push past Carol and Harry, just making it to the employee toilet in time. I puke unceremoniously—this is getting old—and wash up before coming back out to the pharmacy counter.

"Are you okay, hon?" Carol asks with concern. "Are you getting sick?"

I wave my hand in front of my face. "Nah. I feel fine except for being nauseous. Same thing happened yesterday morning and then I was fine for the rest of the day. Maybe it was something I ate."

Carol exchanges a look with her husband. Harry raises his eyebrows at her. Carol reaches under the counter and pulls out a box which she promptly slides across the counter. "Here. You could probably use this."

I reach for the box thinking it's a medication that will help with my tummy troubles. Instead, I discover a pink box with a picture of a woman and a plus sign staring back at me, the words *Pregnancy Test* leaping out from the front.

"I don't need this," I laugh. "It's just something I ate."

Carol shakes her head and points to the bathroom from which I just exited.

Sighing, I scoop up the test. "I'm not...*pregnant*."

On the way to the bathroom I repeatedly tell myself that it's true. I'm *not* pregnant. I can't be pregnant. I'm too young to be pregnant. We're too broke to be pregnant. We've only been married a few years. I don't want to be pregnant...at least not right now.

Once inside the bathroom, I open the box with trembling fingers and pull out the stick inside. I open up the plastic it's wrapped in and proceed to read the instructions—still reminding myself of why I cannot be pregnant.

I pee on the stick as instructed (and my hand as well— not in the instructions). I place the stick on the counter and pull up my pants. Staring at my watch, I drum my fingers on the countertop for three minutes.

With a deep breath, I take a look at the stick, all the while telling myself, *I can't be pregnant.*

Until...I see the faint plus sign.

Crap. I'm pregnant.

1.5

Congratulations! You just found out you're pregnant! You may have been noticing some changes in how you feel, such as morning sickness (a misnomer since it can last all day) and incredible feelings of fatigue. At this point, your baby is the size of a sesame seed, but the heart and lungs are already beginning to develop. Soon, the arms, legs, brain, spinal cord, and nerves will begin to form.

Your feelings right now are likely to run the gamut—you're both excited and nervous about having a baby. After all, you've probably dreamed of having a baby. Still, in nine short months, there will be another person in your life that you are responsible for and that's scary!

You may start to wonder whether the baby is a boy or a girl—some people have a preference, but remember, the most important thing is having a HEALTHY baby. Most likely, you will start to worry about the baby's health and wonder if you will be a good parent...it's okay! These are normal concerns!

There are a lot of changes in store for you over the next few months...both physical and emotional. It can be overwhelming, but luckily, you have The Baby Days website to guide you through this journey! We will give you insights on your pregnancy, month by month to help put you at ease!

****

Before I know what is happening, I find myself at home, sitting at the kitchen table.

I sit there for what feels like hours. Well, it may in fact *be* hours. The sun slips over the horizon while I drum my fingers on the cheap tabletop, lamenting about my current predicament.

I must have forgotten my pill last month. Or this month. I don't know! Am I one month pregnant? Or two months? I can't remember how long it's been. I don't know how these things work. Should I be taking the pill now? Should I make myself throw up the pill from this morning? Should I call someone? Who would I even call? Maybe there's a website or something I can check out...

I turn on the computer, searching for answers to my questions. After some searching, I don't find exactly what I'm looking for, but I do come across a website called The Baby Days that seems to have *some* answers at least. But of course, there is a caveat with each snippet of advice. Call your doctor if you have any questions about your pregnancy.

I get to my feet and find the phone. As I start to dial, I realize I don't know what number I'm dialing. I don't exactly *have* an OB/GYN. I'm going to have to look up a number. *I think we have a phone book somewhere...*

My eye falls on the drawer in the living room where I found the checkbook earlier.

We can't afford a baby! We can barely afford ourselves! What are we going to do?

Thoughts of putting the baby up for adoption run through my mind, until I remember Roger.

That's right! Roger is getting a principal job! Everything will be fine. Wait, wasn't he supposed to call me and let me know how the interview went?

Except he couldn't call me—he had no idea where I was. I had wandered out of the pharmacy after Carol found me in the bathroom, starting at the pee stick with a mixture of repulsion and awe. She had Harry drive me home, and I vaguely remember letting myself into the apartment and slumping into the kitchen chair.

"Amy?" Roger steps through the front door, dumping his bag in the foyer.

I freeze in panic. I haven't worked out in my head what I'm going to say to him. I have no idea how he will react to this sudden and definitely unexpected news.

In fact, we've barely discussed having kids at all. Oh sure we both said we wanted to have them in a pre-wedding, drunken night. I think Roger's exact words were *I'd like to have them eventually.* What does *eventually* mean? Roger *is* older than me—in his late thirties—but maybe he means in his forties. He could even be talking about his fifties. He was never specific.

"In here," I call out to him, even though he obviously can see me standing in the kitchen from the front door.

"Hey," he says as he steps into the kitchen. He leans down and kisses me on the cheek. "Someone on the phone?"

I realize I am still holding the phone in my hand. "Um, no. Wrong number." I force a laugh and hang the phone up.

"I tried to call you at work, but Carol said you had gone home sick. Are you okay?" He takes a step back. "Is it contagious?"

I shake my head. It's definitely *not* contagious. I open my mouth to tell him about the pregnancy test, but something stops me. Roger is running his hands through his hair—he's pale and flushed at the same time. His eyes bear the same look as a deer in headlights. Maybe the interview didn't go as well as he expected.

"It was just a headache," I tell him with a smile that I hope he can't see is fake. "How was the interview?"

He groans and drops into the chair next to me. It creaks in protest. Probably because it is older than I am. We got the kitchen set from my parents when I moved into Roger's apartment. They were getting a new set and my mother was positively appalled when she saw that Roger was sitting on milk crates, and eating off of a makeshift table of sawhorses with a slab of plywood balanced on them.

"Not good?" I wince.

"No, it was okay. They're interviewing a lot more people than I thought. And it seems like they really *love* the mayor's son. At least Joanne Donovan does."

I groan. Joanne Donovan is a member of the school board, infamous district-wide for her cougar-like prowess. She *would* love the mayor's son.

"They said they're not letting us know about their decision until the board meeting. That's two weeks from now. Two weeks is going to be a very long time."

"Really?" He's right. Two weeks *is* a long time. *But you know what else is a long time, Roger? Nine months is a really long time.*

"Yeah. So I'm probably going to be a little on edge for the next couple of weeks." He offers me an apologetic smile before rising to his feet. "I think I'm going to take off this stupid suit and chill out with a beer before dinner. What are we having?"

Either a boy or a girl. I don't know.

I almost say that out loud until I realize that he's talking about dinner. I have not given an iota of thought to what we're having for dinner, considering I have been giving way too much thought to what we're having in nine months. Or eight months. I have no idea how far along I am. Definitely something I should find out.

"Um, how about lemon pepper chicken?" I ask. I see Roger cringe at the suggestion—we have lemon pepper chicken (basically a bottle of marinade poured over chicken) at least once a week, but my cooking skills are severely limited to lemon pepper chicken, beef stir-fry, and English muffin pizzas. I can also boil water for pasta and pour a jar of sauce over it, but Roger really hates that.

"I guess," he says. "As long as there's beer." He opens up the fridge and peers inside. "I guess you didn't have a chance to get the milk, huh?"

I completely forgot about the milk. "I'll go get it after dinner," I tell Roger.

He shakes his head. "No, don't worry about it. I'll go get it now so you can make dinner." He leaves the beer in the fridge and grabs his wallet before walking out the door.

After I hear the front door close, I open the fridge and take out the package of chicken, trying to put Roger's job and this baby and *everything* out of my head. Ripping open the package of chicken, the smell wafts up to my nose and I realize I'm going to be sick again. I dash from the kitchen and once again, make it to the bathroom just in time to puke.

Crap. This is going to be a long nine months.

April

You are 2 months pregnant! In your second month of pregnancy, the embryo is now called a fetus and is the size of a kidney bean. Its heart is beating and you may be able to see that on an ultrasound at this point—it's still too early to hear with a Doppler. Bones, fingers and eyelids are forming. The main organs are forming as well.

Morning sickness and fatigue may start to impede on your daily life. You may find that all you want to do is sleep and you're not hungry enough to eat. You don't look pregnant, but you feel pretty crummy at times. You are wondering if you will ever feel normal again. Rest assured, while these nine months seem long, they are very short in the scheme of things. One day you may look back on your pregnancy in fondness. Try to enjoy every minute.

****

Dear Dr. Herman:

I am contacting your office because I am in need of an OB/GYN and I saw your ad on a pregnancy website. I just found out I am pregnant and I have many questions. And I assume I need to see a doctor anyway, so can I make an

appointment with your office? Can I come in tomorrow? Or Wednesday? Or Friday? Actually, I can come in any day.
Amy Maxwell

Dear Ms. Maxwell:
Please call our office at (555)919-0001. We don't make appointments via email.
Dr. Herman's office

Dear Dr. Herman's office:
Okay, I will call.
Amy Maxwell

Dear Dr. Herman's office:
I called and made an appointment for April 16. That's a long way off. I had a lot of questions for the receptionist but she said she couldn't answer any of them. Can I email you a list of my questions for Dr. Herman to answer?
Amy Maxwell

Dear Ms. Maxwell:
Dr. Herman can answer your questions at your appointment.
Dr. Herman's office

Dr. Herman's office:
But what do I do until then?
Amy

Ms. Maxwell:

*There are many books available that can outline a typical pregnancy, but if you have specific questions, you might try the many baby websites online. The Baby Days is a good one. They will send you monthly updates about your pregnancy and what to expect. Please don't contact us via email. If you should have an **emergency** related to your pregnancy, please call the office.*

Dr. Herman's office

****

I am staring into the fridge two weeks later, trying to decide what will be least likely to cause me throw up. It won't be the chicken. Just the *thought* of chicken, its slippery feel and rubbery taste, makes bile rise up in my throat.

We can't have pasta again. Roger will start asking questions. And I don't have answers. At least not answers he wants to hear.

I lightly touch my belly. I am definitely not ready to tell him about the baby yet. You would think my husband would notice that I throw up at least once a day, and that I look like complete and utter crap. But he really hasn't noticed much about me these past two weeks—he has been completely on edge. He comes home from work, looking all frazzled, like a squirrel looking for a nut in January. Any time the phone rings, he practically leaps from wherever he is sitting and races over to the phone.

Before picking it up, he looks at me and asks, "What if it's the school board?"

And I say, "Then you'll answer it."

Every. Single. Time.

It's never been the school board, though. It's always been my mother. Wanting to know if the school board has called. Which reminds Roger that the school board hasn't called and sets him even more on edge. Oh, the irony.

And I don't really want to talk to my mother either. I am afraid that I will slip and tell her about the baby before I tell Roger. That would definitely not do at all. My conversations with my mother have been very short and to the point lately. I bet she's complaining about how cold and uncaring I am to my sisters.

Also not on my list of pleasant subjects is the fact that I have not been able to ask Harry and Carol for more hours. I've watched Carol nervously chewing her pen cap every time she's been balancing the books in the last two weeks. And Harry has been snapping at anyone who leaves the bathroom light on (mostly me) and mumbling about not owning the electric company.

It seems to me that missing shipment really put the pharmacy in the red. They must really be in dire straits if $3,000 is affecting them this badly. I have started wondering if I may have to look for another job. There's a lot going through my mind, and I don't feel like I have anyone to talk to about it. Least of all Roger.

"There's gotta be something that a pregnant woman can eat without puking," I mumble to myself. "Maybe I can find a recipe or something online." I sit down at the computer on the desk. Roger bought it when he was getting his Master's. It's as slow as hell when you're trying to get on the internet...but then again, that could be our modem. I don't know much about computers other than the fact I can use this one for email and looking up the news and recipes on it. Oh, and I look up the answers to pregnancy questions on The Baby Days website.

After interminable screeching from the modem, I open up my home page to check out the news and I am told by that peppy sounding guy that I have mail. I click on the envelope icon and my email box opens up. Mostly it's junk, but I notice an email from The Baby Days.

Hello Amy! Since you visited our website last week, we thought you might be interested in our chat room, just for expectant moms like you. It's called November Babies and its members are all expecting bundles of joy in November of this year. Ask questions and share your experiences on this journey with like-minded moms. To join a group, go to our website and click on the box in the upper left hand corner.

The Baby Days Team

I stare at the email for a moment before opening a new window and typing in the address for the website. There in the upper left hand corner as promised, are the words November Babies. I click on that and it brings me to another page.

Welcome Moms-to-be!

The Baby Day's Team introduces their brand new chat club...November Babies!

Based on the information you provided on your LMP, we estimate you to be due sometime around the beginning of November. Hang out in our November chat room and meet moms that are going through the same things in their pregnancies that you are. Chat about morning sickness and development stages. Talk about birth plans and dos and don'ts of pregnancy. When your babies are born, you can share birth stories and milestones as well.

I quickly skim the posts that run down the length of the page.

Is it normal to feel sick all day?

The doctor said my baby's heartbeat is fast. What does that mean?

Spotting?

Could I be having twins?

What can I eat?

Can I change the litter box if I use gloves?

Question after question pops up on the screen, followed by answer after answer. Many of those questions were ones that I was wondering myself. I find myself sucked into this little online world of women I don't know at all, living the same life that I'm living right now.

That is until the phone rings and knocks me off line.

I glance at the clock. It's four o'clock. Too early for my mother to be calling—she naps between three-thirty and four-thirty every single day. Sometimes my older sister Beth calls, but it is too early for her as well—she works until well after six. And my sister Joey is probably still sleeping. She stays up and parties most nights and then sleeps till it's time to go out again, much to my parents' delight. Yet, they keep funding her passion projects—photography, interior design, writing, pottery. They (mainly my mother) are convinced that Joey is a prodigy in anything she does and it's just a matter of time before she "breaks out".

It's probably someone trying to sell me something.

I debate about letting the machine get the phone, but in the end, I grab it on the fifth ring.

"Hello?"

"Hello. May I speak with Roger Maxwell, please?"

I recognize the voice on the other end of the phone. It's Joanne Donovan. This phone call is about the job. And Roger is not home.

My heart speeds up as I tell her that Roger isn't home yet.

"Oh. I was hoping to catch him at school at the end of the day, but he wasn't in his classroom. I would have thought he would be home by *now*." She says it with the air of a person who has caught a child in an act of defiance and wants the child to confess before revealing that she's on to him.

"Yes. He coaches the boy's baseball team," I remind her. "They practice immediately after school. Sometimes he's not home until late." I am desperately trying to fluff up Roger's resume for this beotch.

"Oh. That's right." She sounds disappointed, as if she wanted Roger to be up to no good.

"I will give him the message that you called. Is there a number he can reach you at when he gets home?" I ask politely, even though I feel anything but polite.

"No need," she says curtly. "I'm just calling to let him know that we have chosen the candidate for the principal job. It will be official at tonight's board meeting."

Oh wow! Roger got the job!

All the anxiety that built up inside me over the past two weeks suddenly leaves my body in a flood of relief.

We're not going to starve to death! Roger got the job!

"That's wonderful!" I gush. "I'll let him know. I assume he will need to be at the board meeting tonight?" I mentally run through the contents of my closet. I should go to the board meeting as well—what would a principal's wife wear?

There is silence on the other end of the phone.

"What time should I tell him to be there?" I ask. I am still met by silence. "Mrs. Donovan?"

There is a sigh, and finally Joanne Donovan speaks. "Perhaps you misunderstood me Mrs. Maxwell. We chose the candidate for the job. That candidate is *not* Mr. Maxwell. We have chosen Mr. Palmer."

I am certain that I am not hearing her correctly. "Robby Palmer? The mayor's son?"

Mrs. Donovan brightens. "Yes. He was the most qualified candidate. Please let your husband know." She disconnects the call, leaving me holding the phone mid-air. Just as Roger walks in.

"Who was on the phone?" he asks, hope lighting up his face.

Crap, this isn't good.

2.5

Maxwell Mommy: Hi! I'm new here. I'm going to my first doctor appointment today. What should I expect?

Mum 2B: U've come to the right place! Welcome!

Maxwell Mommy: Thanks. I have a lot of questions. This is my first. I'm very nervous about it all and what to expect.

Mom of 3: You should get What to Expect When You're Expecting. I've had three children already. I know what I'm talking about.

She's Having My Baby: Do they make one for dads, too?

Mom of 3: Everything you need to know is in that book.

She's Having My Baby: Well it seems mostly skewed toward the woman.

In a Baby Daze: The woman is the one doing all the work.

She's Having My Baby: I'm going to be a stay at home dad when the baby comes.

In a Baby Daze: You want a medal or a chest to pin it on?

Bun in the Oven: I think it's sweet that he's going to be a stay at home dad! More dad's should do that!

In a Baby Daze: It's "dads", not dad's.

Bun in the Oven: Sorry!

Eating 4 2: I went yesterday. The doctor gave me a list of foods not to eat. I'm so sad.

George's Gal: I'm going to my first appointment today, too! I hope ice cream isn't on that list! I love ice cream.

In a Baby Daze: *Do you realize you have an extremely misogynistic handle "George's Gal"?*
Mom of 3: *Just follow the doctor's advice and everything will be fine.*

****

"Amy Maxwell?" A pretty redheaded nurse is standing in the doorway, charting in hand, smiling at me.

I drop the magazine I am reading, "Pregnancy and You", still recoiling from the overly graphic pictures displayed on virtually every page. I had picked it up looking for something to read while waiting for Dr. Herman, assuming it would be some helpful guide to what to expect in the next nine months. Instead, it was like a horror film, depicting every single unpleasant experience my body would be treated to over the next nine months, and possibly beyond. Apparently there's something called prolapsed uterus that may plague me for the rest of my life.

"Um, yes," I stammer, gathering my bag and placing the magazine back on the stack for some other unsuspecting schmuck find it.

"You can take it with you if you'd like," she tells me in a thick accent. Scottish? Irish, maybe?

I shake my head. "No, that's okay. I was just reading it to pass the time."

With a hearty laugh, she puts her hand on my shoulder. "Scared the life outta ya, did it now?"

"Just a bit."

"I keep telling them they need to get rid of that magazine. It's making all the young lasses terrified of their fate."

I nod my head as she leads me into an exam room and points to a chair. "It definitely did that." I sit and roll up my sleeve.

She offers me a smile as she wraps the blood pressure cuff around my arm. "If it makes ya feel any better, I'm right there with ya." She pats her bulging belly. "Three months along with this wee lass."

"Oh, a girl?" I squeak in a really unnatural high pitched voice, tears springing to my eyes. I have no idea why. What is it about being pregnant that makes me like an emotionally unstable thirteen year old?

"We think. We don't know yet. But I've got three boys at home, so this one better be a girl."

"I think I'm having a boy," I tell her as she slips the stethoscope into her ears.

"Oh ya? Why's that?" she asks, inflating the cuff on my arm.

"Well, I *can't* have a girl," I explain. "I'm one of three girls and my sisters are nuts. I don't think I could handle a girl. I think a boy would be much easier."

The nurse yanks the stethoscope from her ears and starts in on a hearty belly laugh. "Ha ha, you are a rip!"

"What's so funny?" I ask, embarrassed to be laughed at.

"You don't get to choose, lass," the nurse says, wiping the tears from her eyes. "Trust me. I wouldn't have three boys if ya did."

"Oh, I know that," I reply, somewhat indignantly. I'm not a moron. "I'm just saying...if there's a God, he wouldn't give me a girl."

"Oh, there's a God and he has a sense of humor. That's why he gave me three boys. And they're not any easier, by the way. They're just as challenging. Like my sons fed the dog their Easter baskets full of chocolate last weekend."

"Oh no!" I gasp. "Isn't chocolate bad for dogs? Like toxic?"

"Pshaw," the nurse says, waving her hand in front of her face. "This beast would need to eat ten kilos of chocolate to kill him. He's a Sheepdog. It just gave him massive diarrhea. He pooped out all that plastic grass from the baskets, though. That's a bastard to clean up."

"Oh, that's really..." Just the thought of dog poop tainted with green plastic Easter grass is enough to make me want to hurl. My eyes start to well up like they do before I puke.

"Basket?" The nurse holds up the wastebasket from the corner of the room.

I nod just as she sticks the basket under my nose and I let loose into it. I didn't even eat anything this morning, so I have no idea what is coming up. I've taken to not eating until later in the day when I feel *slightly* better, and am able to choke down a yogurt or some saltines without losing it.

"I'm sorry," I tell her, sheepishly wiping my mouth with the tissue she offers me.

"Aye, don't worry about it at all. I've been there myself."

"Still, I'm sorry for making a mess."

"Oh please," she says. "It's nothing compared to the mess we cleaned up yesterday. A mum had a baby right here in this very room."

My eyes widen. "What? That can happen?"

She starts into that hearty belly laugh again. "Oh ya! Happens at least once a month around here. Especially mums who have given birth before. They think they have loads of time but those babes just fly right out of the birth canal. They're slippery little suckers."

Now my eyes pop out of my head—the nurse pats my arm. "Don't worry. Usually doesn't happen with the first one. The first one takes its sweet time and those mums usually go to the hospital too soon. With my first I was in labor for forty-eight whole hours before I got to push. And then I had to push his big Scottish head out for two hours after that. Nearly split me in two, he did. I near collapsed, I did. And he was the easiest delivery of my boys."

I must look like I'm going to puke again because she offers me the bucket. I wave her hand away, unable to speak. I'm not sure this nurse is really the first person an expectant mother should encounter at the doctor's office.

"Okay, well then—" she slides open a cabinet and holds out a paper gown to me. "Put this on, the opening in the front, okay? Dr. Babin will be in shortly."

"Dr. Babin? I thought I was supposed to see Dr. Herman."

"Oh, Dr. Herman is on an emergency. Dr. Babin is filling in for her. You got to get used to that. Happens all the time around these parts."

"Is Dr. Babin a woman?" I had only looked up Dr. Herman's credentials. I had no idea there was another doctor in the practice.

The nurse shakes her head. "Oh no. He's a man."

"Oh." I'm pretty disappointed. I've never had a male OB/GYN. I got my pills from the clinic at college, and I saw a female nurse practitioner. Even though I dropped out, I continued to go there for my pills. Until about five months ago when they caught on to the fact that I wasn't a college student. And now I'm pregnant. Hmmm...coincidence? I think not.

"Dr. Babin is great. You'll love him. He's like a grandpa."

Just as she says that, Dr. Babin hobbles in. Yes, he hobbles. Hunched over. With a cane. Forget grandpa. He's more like a *great*-grandpa.

"Hello, Dr. Babin," the nurse says with a broad grin. "I'm sorry. We got to talking. Mrs. Maxwell isn't in her gown yet."

"Oh, okay Maria. I'll leave her to that. I'll be back in a jiffy," he says as turns on his heel and limps out of the room.

I highly doubt that.

"So get into your gown and I'll be back with the doc," the nurse (Maria) says. "In a *jiffy*," she adds with a twinkle in her eye.

She leaves the room and I quickly change out of my clothes, carefully tucking my underwear underneath my pile of clothes. I barely climb back up on the table when there's a quick rap on the door and it swings open. I pull the gown around my exposed lady bits before someone in the hall sees as Dr.Babin walks in, Maria bringing up the rear.

Gee, he actually wasn't kidding about the jiffy part.

"I'll be in the room during your exam," Maria tells me, scooting over to the side of the room. Dr. Babin lowers himself into the rolling stool at the base of the exam table. It wobbles as he sits—I'm having a horrible vision of the poor little old guy on the floor. But I'm sure Maria would have him on his feet...in a *jiffy*.

"Well, let's see here Mrs. Maxwell. I'm going to start off with a pelvic exam. You'll feel a little cold metal and then some pressure. Try to relax," Dr. Babin says, pulling the miner's helmet over his forehead. Okay, so maybe it's not actually a miner's helmet, but it has a light on the front of it and reminds me of one. It usually makes me giggle. Today is no exception.

What happens next does *not* make me giggle. The cold and the pressure happen all at once. I swear the doctor pinches part of my...*skin*...in the speculum. It has never hurt like this before when I had exams at the clinic. I suck in my breath, trying not to be a big baby.

"Ooopsie," Dr. Babin says. "I think I made a boo boo. Maria, can you get me my glasses?" He retracts the speculum, giving me momentary relief.

Maria reaches into the doctor's coat pocket and retrieves his glasses. She opens them up and perches them on his nose. "Ah, that's better."

Great. I get the doctor who is so old that he can't even see my hoo-ha without his glasses on. How is he going to deliver my kid?

He slides the instrument back in—this time without pinching anything. It still doesn't tickle as he pokes around. Then he pulls it out and practically sticks his whole hand up there instead. I jerk involuntarily. It doesn't hurt, per se, but it's really not comfortable. In fact, it feels like his hand is tickling my tonsils.

I can hear him tell me what he's doing as he's doing it. I'm not sure if that's helpful or it makes everything worse. I really don't want to know about my cervix right now. He staggers to his feet (hand still attached to my crotch) and starts pushing on my abdomen.

I suck in my breath. *Is this normal procedure?* I don't know...I've never been pregnant before. I look to Maria for confirmation. She seems completely uninterested and lost in her own thoughts—probably cataloguing the havoc her sons have wrecked on her house that morning. If she doesn't seem concerned, this must be the process when you're a pregnant patient.

But still, it seems like he's spent an awfully long time up there. Honestly I don't even think Roger spends that much time up there. This is making me feel very squirmy. I am now officially completely uncomfortable because I have a male doctor with his hand up my—

Dr. Babin yanks out his hand and grabs a long and thick stick-like object attached to the computer in the corner of the room. He reaches into the drawer and pulls out what I swear is a condom and rolls it over the stick. Then he takes a tube and squirts gel on it. "I'm going to insert this now," he says. "Relax."

Insert this where—oh, that's where.

It's cold and even more uncomfortable than his hand. I grimace as he yanks it back and forth...probably still looking for those tonsils of mine.

"There you go," he says, pointing at the computer screen.

I squint to see what he's pointing at. It's a blob. With a pulsing blob in the middle.

"Um, okay?" I have no idea what I'm looking at.

"It's your baby," Maria says, jostling my arm like we're best friends sharing a joke or something.

It is?

"That's the heartbeat." Maria points to the pulsing blob in the middle. "That's the head and that's the bottom." She trails her fingers across the screen, pointing these features out to me.

I can't see anything but a white fuzzy patch on the screen. It certainly doesn't look anything like a baby to me. Still, tears well up in my eyes and I feel a surge of maternal pride for this fuzzy patch of blob on the computer screen.

Dr. Babin yanks the stick out of me and throws the condom away. He fiddles with some of the buttons on the computer and it whirls to life, spitting out a piece of paper.

"Here's a picture." Dr. Babin is waving the paper at me. I stare at it, not comprehending any of it. All I can make out is my name on top and today's date.

"Well, congratulations Mrs. Maxwell." Dr. Babin stands and pulls off his gloves, dropping them into the waste basket that I threw up in not that long ago. "You are indeed pregnant."

There was a doubt in this guy's mind?

"Um, okay. Thanks?"

He picks up my chart, sits back down in the wobbly chair, and starts pawing through it, making murmuring noises for a few minutes. Then he just stares into space, no more murmuring noises either. I quickly check his chest to reassure myself that he is actually breathing. Once again, Maria doesn't look concerned. She's probably wondering what to make for dinner.

Suddenly Dr. Babin leaps to his feet. "Okay, then!" He pokes the air with his finger, startling me and Maria as well. "So Mrs. Maxwell...you're about eight weeks along. You'll be coming in for visits every eight weeks until you are twenty-four weeks along. Then you'll come in every four weeks until thirty-two weeks, and then every two weeks until thirty-six. After that you'll come once a week until delivery. Make sure you make an appointment with the front desk for your next appointment before you leave."

I nod numbly, head spinning. I wish I had thought to bring a notebook or something to write this all down. "Um, okay."

"Any other questions?" he asks, grandfatherly smile on his face.

Um, about a million?

"Dr. Babin," Maria interjects. "You need to tell her when she's due so she can let the front desk know when to make the appointments for."

"Yes, that's correct!" Dr. Babin replies, poking the air once more.

He grabs a wheel that's sitting on the counter and spins it. He makes those murmuring noises again and says, "Mrs. Maxwell, you're going to be a mother around the beginning of November. Maybe the baby will be a few days early and you can have a Halloween baby. That's nice. My oldest is a Halloween baby."

The room starts to spin and as I fall back onto the exam table, print-out in hand. I knew I was pregnant, but it still hadn't dawned on me until he said it.

Crap, I'm going to be a mother.

3

May

You are 3 months pregnant! Your baby is about the size of a plum. You are nearing the end of the first trimester so your baby has all his or her organs now. Fingernails are developing! Your baby is moving his or her tiny limbs, but you won't feel it yet. You are probably still nauseous and tired, but the good news is that may start to get better soon. (It also may not—some women are nauseated their entire pregnancy Let your doctor know if this is the case for you.)

When your appetite returns, you may feel as if you are gaining a lot of weight—perhaps your pants don't fit as well—but hold off on buying the maternity clothes just yet. Even though the risk of miscarriage decreases at this point, it is better to wait until you have seen your doctor to make sure everything is moving along smoothly to announce your pregnancy.

****

I suck in my gut. I try lying on the bed. I try sucking in my gut a little more. I roll off the bed and grab a metal coat hanger (I saw it in a movie once). I attempt to use the coat hanger to pull my zipper up.

It is no use. There is no way that I am going to get my jeans zipped.

Letting all the air out of my belly, I sit up, completely deflated. I can't believe how fat I've gotten. Yes, yes, I know I'm pregnant. But I don't look or feel pregnant. I just look and feel fat.

But, in a way, not looking pregnant is a good thing. Because even though I am almost three months along, I haven't told Roger about the baby yet.

Please don't stone me.

Ever since he got the phone call that he didn't get the principal job, he's been *so* bummed out. And yes, I thought about telling him I'm pregnant in the hopes that it cheers him up and gives him something to look forward to—but what if it doesn't? What if it makes him even more bummed out?

Plus, now that I know there are money problems, I've been noticing that he's been staring at the checkbook and our bank statements a little more intensely. He's been looking much more pained than usual when a bill arrives. And he's definitely been trying to cut back on spending. (He put a brick in the toilet to reduce our water bill last week—I don't think that's going to help.)

And I *was* going to talk to Harry and Carol about more hours, but every time I get up the nerve to ask, it seems that Carol starts telling me a story about how their revenue is down or how prices have gone up. It's just never been a good time.

I stare at the ultrasound printout that I've stashed in my underwear drawer and make a decision. Today, I'm determined to do everything I've been putting off. I'm going to have to ask for more hours. *And* I'm going to tell Roger about the baby.

I have another doctor's appointment in a few days and I really want Roger to be there. And he can't very well be there if I don't tell him about the baby. I figure maybe if I can tell him that I'm going to get more hours at work that will soften the blow of the whole surprise pregnancy thing. *Maybe.*

Realizing that there is no way in hell I'm going to fit in these jeans, I yank them off and reach for a pair of stretch pants. They've been getting a lot of use lately and they're starting to get stretched out in places that shouldn't be stretched out. Like my butt. I check that my underwear isn't a bright color or full of designs before pulling on the stretch pants.

I'm going to have to get some maternity clothes soon as well. Except, we probably can't afford for me to go out and go on a shopping spree. *Well, buying a few pairs of jeans hardly constitutes a spree*, I rationalize with myself. *We're not destitute...or homeless.* Yet.

I pull on a top, thanking God that at least my shirts still fit. My boobs have become ginormous in the last month. And still, Roger hasn't noticed. Which is exactly how I know he's really in a bad place mentally. I'm pretty sure my boobs are the first thing Roger noticed about me when we met. In fact, I often tease him by reminding him that he spent the entire night we met talking to my boobs and not looking me in the eye. He claims he was just shy. Yeah, right.

I stop in the bathroom to run a brush through my hair and briefly contemplate brushing my teeth. Deciding that I do *not* want to gag and throw up this morning, I quickly rinse with mouthwash instead. Yeah, I know. If you told me three months ago that I would skip brushing my teeth on a regular basis, I would have told you that you were nuts. However, the last month or so has been completely out of the ordinary.

Besides Roger's constant moping, there's been the depressing fact I haven't been able to go one solid day without puking for *some* reason. And some of those reasons (like brushing my teeth and bending down to tie my shoe) are so stupid that I can't believe they're causing me to be ill. And they're part of my every day routine (obviously), so it's been difficult to get around them.

Plus, I'm so exhausted that I can barely keep my eyes open at times. Two days ago I was driving to the grocery store and fell asleep at a stoplight. Yesterday I fell asleep standing at the kitchen counter waiting for my waffle to finish toasting. And no, Roger didn't notice that either.

I shove my feet into a pair of tennis shoes without laces (I'm not risking bending down today) and shuffle out the door to work. Because I have no laces in my shoes, I'm nervous about walking two blocks to the pharmacy—what if I trip and fall? I don't think that would be good for the baby...or me. Plus, it looks like it's going to rain soon.

Instead of walking, I opt to drive old Bessie. I poke the key into the lock and miraculously manage to get it unlocked on the first try. Due to the rust build-up inside the lock, it sometimes takes quite a while to get the door unlocked, which is one of the reasons that I don't like to drive the darn car. And it stalls when making a left hand turns, which is absolutely terrifying. I usually have to go out of my way to only make right hand turns.

I lower myself into the car and the springs in the seat immediately assault my backside—reminding me of yet *another* reason that I hate to drive the car. I put the key in the ignition and the car immediately dings angrily at me. I look down at the dashboard and discover that I am pretty much out of gas.

"Crap."

The pharmacy is only a few blocks away and I *should* be able to make it. Of course, with my luck, one never knows. I putter around the block, as if going slower will somehow make the gas last longer.

It must be my lucky day because not only do I make it to work without running out of gas, I manage to find a parking spot right in front of the building. In the two years since I started working here, I don't think I have ever found a parking spot right in front of the building.

As I step out of the car, I narrowly miss stepping in a pile of dog poop in the middle of the street, causing me to wonder how a dog poops in the *middle* of the street. Just as I step through the front door, the skies open up, and I miss getting drenched by seconds.

But that's where my lucky streak completely ends.

When I enter, Carol is looking completely forlorn behind the counter, Harry peering over her shoulder at the piece of paper she holds in her hand. They hear the bell over the door jingle as I enter—Carol drops the paper and Harry looks up. Harry turns away and runs his hand nervously through his graying hair.

"Let me know if you...well, just...good luck," he mumbles to Carol as he turns and retreats to the shelves of pills.

Carol scowls at his back, but as I approach, her scowl turns to a sad smile. "Hi, Amy."

"Everything okay?" I ask, stowing my purse under the counter. Carol shuffles the papers on the counter uncomfortably, avoiding my eye. From behind the stacks of pills, I hear Harry clear his throat. "Carol?"

She sighs and wrings her hands. "Can you come in the back room with me?"

"Uh, yeah. Of course." I follow Carol as she weaves in between the shelves to reach the cramped little room in the back of the pharmacy.

This is where she does most of her accounting work and ordering. It's where I know that I can find her if she's not in the front of the store helping customers. There is a desk, two chairs, and several filing cabinets in this room.

Carol lowers herself into her desk chair. "Have a seat," she says, gesturing to the other chair next to her desk. I sit, suddenly feeling incredibly claustrophobic. The only other time I've *sat* in this room has been the day I interviewed for the job. I usually just stand in the doorway when I'm talking to Carol. This *sitting in the chair* seems so...formal.

"Is everything okay, Carol?" I'm not sure I want to know the answer to that question, but I need to know why I'm here, in this tiny room, *sitting* in a chair. She's fiddling with some paper clips on her desk, not looking at me.

"Well, not really," Carol says, finally looking up. "You know how we've been wondering what's going in the building on the corner?"

Of course I know. *Everyone's* been wondering that. There is an abandoned building on the corner of East Street and Yardley Ave. It was once a small mom and pop grocery store that went out of business years ago. It sat abandoned for a decade, until this winter when construction crews arrived to fix the place up. A giant partition had gone around the building as well, making the progress, and the nature of the eventual business going in the building, a secret. A sign went on the marquee not too long ago, but it too was covered up in secret.

"Yes, of course. Did you find out what it was?"

Carol grimaces as if she is in pain. "It's going to be a Wal-Drugs."

It's like all the air has left the room. "A Wal-Drugs? That big box store slash pharmacy combo that they opened in Mercer not too long ago?" I gasp out.

Mercer is the next town over. The Wal-Drugs they opened a few months ago is new and shiny—some of our customers have even moved their accounts to the Wal-Drugs, prompting Harry and Carol to worry about losing customers. It hadn't come to fruition though because not too many people wanted to travel the twenty minutes to reach the Wal-Drugs in Mercer.

At least I thought it hadn't. Maybe that's why Carol had been stressing over finances for the last few weeks or so. Maybe we had lost a lot more customers than I thought. And now if they were opening a Wal-Drugs in town, we would lose a lot more customers for sure.

Carol nods in response to my question. "Yes. And many customers have already transferred their accounts. We're anticipating a sixty percent loss of revenue after they open."

"Sixty percent? That's insane!" I am quickly doing the math. I don't know anything about accounting, but I doubt that Harry and Carol can sustain a revenue loss that large.

"It is," Carol agrees. "We're hoping it's not as bad as that because we would definitely need to close. Unfortunately, we're going to have to let all our employees go." She says this while staring down at her hands folded neatly on the desk. It takes me a second to register exactly what she's telling me.

They have to let the employees go. I'm an employee. Wait! They have to let me go?

The air in the room is completely gone now and I feel like an elephant is standing on my chest.

If they let me go, I can't ask for more hours. If I can't ask for more hours, we're going to be broke! We're never going to make it! Oh my God! We're going to be living in a cardboard box! On the street! Or worse...we'll have to move in with my parents!

The pregnancy hormones are wreaking havoc on my system as it is—the new revelation that I am jobless causes me to burst out in tears. Which causes Carol to burst into tears. She rushes from behind the desk and wraps her arms around me. I sit in the chair like a lump, numbly crying, not reacting to her hug.

"Oh you poor thing, I'm so sorry to have to do this to you when you're pregnant!" she sobs. This makes me cry harder. Which makes Carol cry harder.

"Is everything okay in here?" Harry is standing in the doorway, staring at the two hysterical females in his pharmacy. We don't answer him and he slinks away, probably not wanting to deal with either of us. That's how Harry is—background scenery. Carol is the heart and soul of this pharmacy. The heart and soul that I will have to leave.

She pulls away and gazes at me like a loving mother trying to ease her daughter's first heartbreak.

"If it helps, we're not letting anyone go till the end of the month. Wal-Drugs opens next week, and we're hoping to keep it afloat for a few weeks. That'll give you time to find something else."

I groan and wave my hand at my belly. "Who's going to hire a pregnant woman?"

"It's illegal to refuse to hire someone because they're pregnant. Besides, you don't have to tell them you're pregnant until after they hire you," Carol says with a mischievous smile. "No one can tell you're pregnant, honey."

"Yeah, not even my husband," I grumble.

Carol's eyes widen. "You haven't told him yet?"

I shake my head. "He didn't get the principal job. I think he's worried about money, so I didn't want to tell him yet." I bite my lip so I don't cry—I don't want to cry anymore. I'm getting a headache from crying so much.

Carol's face crumbles. "Oh damn. This is really not a good time, is it? I feel terrible!"

I wipe my tears from my cheeks and shake my head. "It's not your fault, Carol." *I f*eel terrible for upsetting her.

"You know I would keep you if I could, right?" She eyes me with concern, as if I would ever doubt her.

I nod, not able to form words without my voice cracking.

"Trust me. I would keep you over Harry if I could."

This causes me to chuckle...*slightly*.

"Amy! Carol!" Harry is calling nervously from the front. "Customers!" He's going to hate having to deal with customers when I'm gone. He's very un-peoply.

Carol straightens herself up and smooths down her hair. She grabs a tissue from the box on the desk and dabs at her eyes. "Does it look like I've been crying?"

"Not at all," I lie, offering her a weak smile.

She knows I'm lying to her. "Thanks, honey."

"Amy! Carol!" Harry calls out impatiently.

"Coming! Keep your shirt on!" Carol calls out. She leans down and plants a kiss on the top of my head before leaving.

I'm left alone in the little cramped room with no job (in a month) and no money.

Crap. I need to find a job.

3.5

Maxwell Mommy: So I need to tell my husband about the baby. Any ideas how I should do it?

Bun in the Oven: I told my husband by putting a cinnamon bun in the oven and asking him to take it out :)

Maxwell Mommy: That's a cute idea! I'll have to see if I can find any cinnamon buns.

Mom of 3: Make sure you don't eat raw dough. You could get salmonella.

Eating 4 2: What about raw cookie dough?

Mom of 3: No raw cookie dough! Call your doctor if you've eaten raw cookie dough!

In a Baby Daze: You didn't tell your husband yet? You're three and a half months pregnant!

Mum 2B: Don't they recommend that you don't tell anyone until the 2nd trimester? I only told my mum this week.

She's Having My Baby: Not the baby's father! I'd be ticked off if my wife didn't tell me she was pregnant till then.

Maxwell Mommy: Well there was a reason I didn't tell him. I lost my job and he didn't get the job wanted. He's upset and I don't want him to be worrying about money right now.

George's Gal: Oh no Maxwell Mommy! That's terrible.

In a Baby Daze: So you're broke? Ugh. I can't stand people having babies that can't afford to. Are you living on government assistance?

Maxwell Mommy: *No! We're not broke. And I'm looking for a new job right now.*
Mum 2B: *Good luck!*

****

A few days later, I am sitting at the kitchen table, pouring over the classified ads. Roger left for work early today. He's been working his tail off between coaching the baseball team and working on a curriculum committee. He took that job the other day and told me that it was good money. He did not add the fact that we really, *really* need good money. But I know the truth. I snuck a peek at the checking account statement after he opened it yesterday, and it is even more dire than before. There are ten dollars in the account.

It's T minus twenty-something days until I am jobless, so I am going to find a job before we are living in that cardboard box. And before I have to tell Roger about losing my job. I know him—he will totally stress himself out taking on even more extra work to make ends meet. He's a pretty proud, self-made kind of guy. He would probably rather live in that cardboard box than live with my parents.

Oh, and I've got to get another job before I tell him about the baby—that would definitely put him over the edge. As much as I wanted him to come to my doctor appointment this week, I went by myself, still not ready to tell him about the baby.

I'm taking a sip of my tea when my eye falls on an ad from the ACC—animal control center. It appears as if they are opening a brand new shelter—right here in town. They are hiring for all positions. And the pay? Almost twice the amount I get now at the pharmacy. This is perfect! I love animals!

I grab a pen and paper, and quickly jot down the phone number before I haul my ever expanding ass out of the chair and waddle over to the phone. Okay, maybe I'm exaggerating *slightly*, but ever since I got my appetite back, I've been stuffing my face.

Without even thinking about what I am going to say, I dial the number from the classified ad. After two rings, a brusque woman answers the phone.

"ACC. Amanda."

That's it. She doesn't say what her job title is or ask where she may direct my call. Just…Amanda.

"Um, hi, Amanda. My name's Amy Maxwell. I saw the ad in the paper for—"

"Are you a certified animal control officer?" she asks, cutting me off.

"Um, no, but the ad said that—"

"The pay mentioned in the ad is only for certified animal control officers. The rate for all other positions is minimum wage. Non-negotiable."

My heart sinks a little. Had I known that, I wouldn't have called. I would have continued to look for another opportunity. Still, I made the phone call and I'm already on the phone with this rude woman. I might as well get an interview.

"Um, okay. Can I apply?"

"You have to apply in person at our trailer on the corner of Fifth and Washington Street. Our new building doesn't open until next week. We're taking applications Wednesday through Friday, nine am through noon *only*. And we're only accepting applications *this* week. It doesn't matter how qualified you think you are, we will not accept any applications after this week." She does not sound even remotely sympathetic about this fact.

I glance over at the calendar. It's Friday, the last day they're accepting applications. And it's already eleven o'clock in the morning. I have exactly one hour to get dressed and over to the trailer on the corner of Fifth and Washington. Well, actually, even less. I have a feeling it's going to take me a few minutes to actually fill out the application—and I have an even stronger feeling that this woman won't take the application from me a second past noon.

"Okay, I'll be there in twenty minutes!" I hang up the phone and inspect my pajama pants to make sure that they are passable for regular pants. Considering I sleep in leggings most of the time (so stretchy over my ever expanding waistline…) they will have to do. I pull off my oversized top (which will *not* do because I dripped my runny eggs all over the front of it while trying to eat—and my belly isn't even that big yet!), and dash into the bedroom to replace it.

Peering into the closet, I realize I have not gotten a chance to wash clothes in a while and my choices are limited. Everything is either too small on me (with my ginormous boobs—I have no idea how Roger hasn't noticed those yet) or too heavy. It's pretty warm out for May.

In a fit of desperation, I grab one of Roger's button down shirts. Hey, they're in style. In fact, I don't look too bad in his shirt, I realize as I button it up. And yes, it buttons over my giant boobs. It reaches past my giant butt, too.

After I slip my feet into a pair of open-toed sandals, ignoring the fact that I have not had a pedicure in over six months, I peek at myself in the mirror. It's not a pretty sight, but I don't have time to worry about it. I don't even have time to obsess over the fact that my hair is in an untidy bun on top of my head. This interview is just practice for when I find a better job in the classifieds. I quickly brush my teeth and swipe lip gloss over my mouth before grabbing my purse and running out the door.

When I reach the parking lot, I groan, realizing that I'm going to have to take the car. There is no way I'll make it across town on foot before noon. With minimal effort, I manage to get the door to open on the first try and toss my bag on the front seat. I start up the car and reverse out of the parking spot—without looking in my rearview mirror—and promptly hear a sickening thud.

My heart lurches and I am hot and dizzy, like I'm going to puke. *Please don't be a person, please don't be a person...*

Hands trembling, I push open the car door, which makes a horrible squeaking noise. I cover my eyes—I don't want to look, but I know I *have* to look. Steeling my nerves for a kid on a bike under my tires, I creep around the back of the car and peek.

There is garbage strewn everywhere on the grass—and a puppy.

"Oh my God! I hit a puppy!"

I'm appalled and nauseated—I throw up on the grass next to the puppy. She promptly leaps to her feet and comes over to inspect the mess I've made. She peers up at me, cocking her head to the side—she's breathing fine and she doesn't look like she's bleeding. She seems to be limping, but doesn't act like she's in pain. Honestly, she looks perfectly fine.

"How is that possible?" I wonder out loud. And then I see that on the other side of the car lies a metal garbage can on its side. With a nice dent in it. A dent that matches the one on my bumper. The thud I heard was the garbage can toppling over, not me hitting the puppy.

I am so relieved that I almost puke again. *Just when I was getting rid of this morning sickness thing!*

The puppy, cuddly and fat, waddles over to me and paws at my pants leg. She whimpers and gazes up at me with her chocolatey puppy dog eyes. My heart, of course, melts and I start to tear up. I'm a hormonal animal lover...what else was going to happen?

I scoop the puppy into my arms and continue to inspect her for damage, making certain that I did not hit her with the car. I also look around her neck, in hopes there is a collar and tags so I can see who she belongs to, but there are none. The puppy thinks we are playing a game and nips at my hands.

"No, no, no," I tell her with a chuckle. I lean into the car and lower her onto the passenger side seat. "You're in luck today, missy. I'm on the way to the animal shelter. I'll take you with me, and we'll figure out who you belong to."

The puppy cocks her head to the side and lets out a little squeaking noise, as if she understands what I'm saying.

I climb into the driver's side and *carefully* pull away this time. Glancing at the clock on the dashboard, I see that I only have a half an hour to get downtown and fill out the application before the noon deadline. I hope that Amanda, the woman on the phone, is at least remotely understanding about the fact that I needed to stop and bring the stray puppy in. After all, she works in an animal shelter. You would think she has a heart, right? At least for animals, anyway.

As I drive, the puppy props her paws up on the door and leans toward the glass, fascinated with the sights passing by the window. Her tail is docked, but she wags her little nubbin of a tail eagerly, further pulling at my very hormonal heart-strings.

I wipe tears from my eyes as we make it to the trailer on the corner of Fifth and Washington in record time, without any further incidents. I find a parking spot right out front and scoop the puppy back into my arms. "Come on, missy. Let's find out who you belong to."

I enter the trailer with the wriggling puppy in my arms. It's a cramped space, so I immediately encounter a desk with an unpleasant young woman behind it.

"This is not the shelter," she informs me with a scowl. "You need to bring animals that you are surrendering to the shelter, not here. And you need to fill out an application. You can't just dump an animal."

Judging by the voice, I can tell that this is Amanda, the super pleasant woman I spoke to not too long ago.

"Oh, I'm not looking to surrender her. I found her on the side of the road." I don't mention the fact that I thought I hit her with my car.

The woman rolls her eyes and tosses her hair over her shoulder with a huff. "Do you see any cages for animals here? You still need to go to the old shelter—"

"I know, but I was on my way here to fill out an application. I called about a half hour ago? Amy Maxwell?"

Amanda looks like she A. has no recollection of that conversation, and B. couldn't care less even if she did.

"Anyway," I continue, setting the puppy down on the floor, "you said that you weren't taking any applications after noon, so I didn't want to be late. I figured the puppy could wait with me while—"

"You assumed? You know what happens when you *assume*?"

"I—" I start to open my mouth to tell this woman that I didn't say I *assumed* anything, when a high pitched squeal reaches my ears.

"Oh my God! How adorable!"

A tall woman with gorgeous red curly hair is emerging from a door at the back of the trailer. She practically drops to her knees in the doorway. I watch the puppy's entire body wag as she runs to the woman's outstretched arms. "What a *gorgeous* ball of fluff!"

"Um, thanks?" I'm not sure how to answer. The dog isn't mine, but I feel somewhat responsible for her adorableness. I did almost hit her with my car after all.

"Is she yours?" the woman asks as the puppy proceeds to cover her face in kisses.

"No, actually I was bringing her in because she was wandering around the parking lot of my apartment complex and I don't know who she belongs to. She doesn't have tags."

And I didn't want her to get hit by another wacko backing into garbage cans.

"Oh, this isn't the shelter, though," the woman says with dismay.

"I *told* her that," Amanda pipes up, triumphantly. "She came in here for a job application. *And* brought a dog. Like we have cages or something lying around here in this tiny trailer." Amanda adds a snort and rolls her eyes.

The other woman does not share her feelings on the matter, however. "Oh wow! That's wonderful!" she gushes, still being enthusiastically licked to death by the puppy.

"What's wonderful?" Amanda asks, scowl deepening her face.

"That she's here for an application. Did you fill it out already?" she asks me.

"Um, no, I didn't get to—"

Amanda cuts me off. "We're only accepting applications until noon. It's already eleven fifty-four—"

The curly-haired woman waves her off. "Oh, don't be ridiculous. You know she's been the only normal human being to show up for the position." She turns toward me and says, "The last guy listed his address as *The Bridge where the Billy Goats Gruff live.* We've had some winners. The money is crap."

She hands me the puppy. "Amanda, give her an application."

"But Bridget, I—"

She ignores Amanda's protests and smiles warmly at me. "When you're done with it, I'll interview you, but it'll just be a formality. I can tell you'll be perfect for the job."

"Oh. Okay." I'm not sure what to make of this. Or the puppy. It's going to be a little difficult to fill out an application with a puppy in my arms.

"And Amanda, call Troy and have him pick up the puppy in the dog catcher's van and bring her to the shelter."

"Troy?" Amanda practically squeaks. "Um, yes. Of course. Right away." She grabs the phone off the desk. I don't know much about this woman, but I can guess that she may just enjoying seeing this Troy. And I don't feel particularly generous toward her. Plus, I gaze at the puppy's chocolate brown eyes and I can't envision her riding around in the back of a dog catcher's van.

"Don't worry about it," I say sweetly. "I'll drop her off myself when I'm done here."

Amanda opens her mouth to protest, but Bridget says, "Wonderful. I'll be waiting for you in the back when you're ready Miss…." She holds her hand out to me, expectant look on her face. It's apparent that she's waiting for me to tell her my name.

"Maxwell. Amy Maxwell."

Bridget nods. "Great to meet you, Amy Maxwell. I'm Bridget Lowry. Can't wait to have you on board."

She waves before heading to the back of the trailer, leaving me with the puppy...and a scowling Amanda.

Amanda shoves the application at me. "I hope you have a pen," she snaps, before turning her attention back to the computer.

I dig through my purse and think, *Crap, I'm going to have to work with this girl.*

****

The script at dinner that night goes something like this:

Me: How was work today?

Roger: Tiring. The team looks like garbage. I'm going to have to hold practice for longer tomorrow. We can't possibly go to states looking like this.

What a perfect segue!

Me: Speaking of *garbage*, I hit a garbage can today.

Roger: (poking at a piece of lemon chicken) You what?

Me: (poking at a piece of lemon chicken and wanting to fling it across the room) Hit a garbage can backing out of the parking lot.

Roger: (slapping forehead) Is there anything wrong with the car?

Me: (cringing) A *small* dent. But the good news is I didn't hit the puppy.

Roger: (holding piece of lemon chicken mid-air) *What* puppy?

Me: The puppy in the parking lot.

Roger: (lowering fork) Where is this puppy?

Me: (nonchalantly) At the animal shelter.

Roger: (breathing a sigh of relief) Okay. Well. Take the car to Joe at Ramm's Autobody tomorrow. He can give us an estimate to bang out the dent. We never got it fixed after your accident, so maybe he can bang that dent out, too. And we might as well get that lock fixed. We've been putting it off forever. (Spears a piece of lemon chicken and begins chewing)

A Few Minutes Later:

Me: I lost my job.

Roger: (spits out piece of lemon chicken) You what????

Me: Lost my job. The pharmacy is downsizing because of the Wal-Drug opening in town.

Roger: (grabbing paper bag to hyperventilate into) Oh God. Don't take the car to the mechanic now. You'll have to live with the dent. Where's the phone? I'm going to call Fred and see if they need a yearbook committee advisor. Or maybe I can coach the girls' volleyball team. Or maybe sweep up after the track meets and the school play.

Me: It's okay.

Roger: How can it possibly be okay? (breathes into paper bag)

Me: I got another job!

Roger: (lowers paper bag) Where?

Me: (cutting up lemon chicken and moving it around the plate) Um...the new animal shelter that's opening next week.

Roger: The same animal shelter you brought the puppy you hit with the car?"

Me: I didn't hit the puppy with the car. I hit a *garbage can*. And yes. The same animal shelter.

Roger: Oh boy. Don't go bringing any animals home. We can't afford an animal.

Me: I won't bring any animals home. I promise.

And Another Few Minutes Later...

Me: Oh, and I'm pregnant by the way.

Roger: You're *what*?

Me: I'm pregnant.

Roger: (now hyperventilating into the paper bag) How can you be pregnant?

Me: Well you see when a man loves a woman—

Roger: That's not what I meant, Amy! I know *how!* I thought you were on the Pill!

Me: It apparently did not work. I also may have forgotten to take it a time or two…

Roger: Amy! How can you be so irresponsible! I'm not ready to be a father!

Me: Oh stop! You're thirty-seven years old! No one thinks they're ready to be a parent! If people waited till they were ready, the human race would die out!

Roger: How are we going to afford a baby? (grabs my hands) Amy, we're broke.

Me: I know, Roger. I saw the checkbook. That's why I wanted to get a job right away. That's why I took the first job I got.

Even though I'll have to work with evil Amanda.

Roger: I'm going to teach summer school.

Me: Oh Roger, you hate summer school.

Roger: I don't really have a choice, now do I? *Someone* got pregnant.

Me: (annoyed) I didn't do this alone, did I?

Roger: I'm sorry, Amy. I didn't want to be like this. Forgive me. You're right. I'm thirty-seven years old. I should be able to provide for you and a baby and I can't. What kind of man can't provide for his family? (dropping head in hands)

This is where the whole conversation goes completely off script...

Is he crying? I don't think I've ever seen him cry! Well, except when his beloved Mets lost the World Series. That was a rough night.

It breaks my heart that Roger feels inadequate. He's not, by any stretch of the imagination. In fact, he impresses me with the lengths he will go to in order to ensure my happiness. Heck, he never even told me we were having money problems until I just dropped this baby bomb in his lap. He wanted to shield me from it.

Leaving my chair, I crouch down at his side and pull his hands away from his face. He looks up at me and there are indeed tears glistening in his eyes.

"Roger, you do more than provide for me. It's my fault that we don't have enough money. I should have finished college. I would have a better job right now, and we wouldn't be in this situation. I'm the one who should be sorry. And you're a great husband. And you're going to be an even better dad."

That makes his eyes widened. "Oh my God. I'm going to be a dad." He reaches for the paper bag to hyperventilate again. "A little person is going to be counting on me."

"And me," I remind him. This is a joint effort. It's going to be fine. It's going to be *great*."

He gazes at me skeptically. "You think so?"

I nod. "It is. And in a few weeks, I have an appointment scheduled. They're going to do an ultrasound. So we can see the baby on the screen."

His eyes widen. "They can do that?"

I laugh. "Yeah, silly. It's the twenty-first century now. Where have you been?"

"Stuck in a school with a bunch of teenagers." His eyes cloud over. "Oh God. We're going to have teenager."

"Um, not yet. Relax. We still have to get through having a baby."

"Yeah, we do!" Roger leaps to his feet, practically knocking me over. "Amy! You shouldn't be squatting on the floor like that! Come sit on the couch! Put your feet up!" He pulls me to my feet and practically drags me over to the couch.

I'm laughing as he pulls my arm. "I'm fine, Roger! I'm pregnant, not an invalid."

"But you need to rest. Sit, sit." He points at the couch like I'm a guest. "Maybe you shouldn't work at the animal shelter. That might be too strenuous in your condition."

"Oh my God, Roger! I'm not in a *condition!*"

He's not listening to me as he starts babbling.

"We have to child-proof the apartment and get a better car and get baby gates and take prenatal classes and oh, we have to tell your mom and dad and your sisters."

I cringe. "Can we skip that part?"

"I think they'll notice something is up when you're as big as a house."

"What? I'm not going to be as big as a house!"

"Yes you are. I'm going to make you eat all the nutritious food in the world so we have a perfect baby." He kneels down at my side. He is practically glowing. I actually haven't seen him this excited...well, since his beloved Mets were in the pennant race.

"As long as it's ours, it'll be perfect," I tell him as I gaze into his eyes. I don't think I've felt this amorous since...well, said perfect baby was planted in his or her current spot.

Roger leans forward to kiss me and...

(Nothing to see here. This is a PG version of my life...)

Crap. I have to tell my mother I'm pregnant.

4

June

You are 4 months pregnant. Your baby is about the size of a pear. The baby's nervous system is functioning at this point in time. Eyelids and fingernails are formed. He or she may begin to suck their thumb. Your doctor may actually be able to determine the sex in the next couple of weeks. You've gotten your appetite back and you're probably not as tired. You may be starting to wear maternity clothes at this point in time because you'll find that your regular clothes are not up to the challenge of your expanding waistline. You look pregnant and are starting to glow!

This is the second trimester, the honeymoon phase of the pregnancy. However, it's not without its problems. Due to increased blood volume, you may be finding that you are prone to nosebleeds or bleeding gums. These are both common symptoms, but be sure to speak with your doctor if you are concerned.

Enjoy this precious time of your pregnancy! It won't last long.

****

The next week, I pick up the phone, hands shaking. Roger gave me three tasks this week. Call the mechanic about my car, get more milk and peanut butter, and call my mom to tell her about the pregnancy.

I have completed the first two task with far less trepidation than this last task—even though the mechanic said it would be five hundred dollars to fix everything that was wrong with my car, including the garbage can sized dent in the rear bumper. I have actually been avoiding calling my mother for as long as humanly possible, but it's Friday and Roger is going to get annoyed if I don't tell her before the weekend.

The phone rings five times before my mother picks up. I'm actually about to hang up when I hear her voice.

"Amy?" She sounds groggy and confused. I called her right in the middle of her nap. This was not an accident. I was really hoping the machine would pick up and I wouldn't actually have to have this conversation with her. I am panting and have broken out into a sweat.

I take in a lungful of air before speaking.

"Hi, Mom just wanted to call you and let you know you're going to be a grandmother sometime in November okay bye now!" I slam the phone down before my mother can answer. I briefly consider disconnecting it. And changing my number.

Obviously I don't do either of these things quickly enough because as soon as I hang up the phone, it is ringing. My mother must have me on speed dial.

"Amy Francine Maxwell! How dare you hang up the phone on me! After saying something like that!"

I cringe. *How can she still reduce me to the emotional equivalent of a chastised ten year old?* "Sorry, Mom. I think we got disconnected accidentally." We *did* get disconnected.

I was just the one doing the disconnecting. And it was not accidentally at all.

"Amy, what did you just say to me? Did you say something about being a grandmother?"

"Ah, yeah...congrats! Gotta go—" I try to hang up the phone but my mother's sharp voice on the other side prevents me from doing so. I start to put the phone back up to my ear, but she's screaming so loudly that I'm afraid she will rupture my eardrum. Screaming with what sounds like...*joy*?

This was absolutely not the reaction I was expecting from her. I was expecting the typical *Oh Amy we're so disappointed in you* response that I usually get when I do something—like get married. Or drop out of college. Or pretty much everything I've ever done my whole life that doesn't measure up to Beth.

"I'm so excited, Amy!" my mother squeaks when she finally stops screaming. *Did I dial my real mother or is this a stand-in?*

"Frank! Frank!" She starts calling for my father. I hear her breathlessly running with the cordless phone in her hand, heels clacking on the hardwood floor.

"What is Dad doing home already?" My father is usually at his job as a police detective from nine in the morning till about five o'clock. And sometimes the urgency of his cases or new developments having him working even longer hours.

I am met with silence. Even her heels stop clacking.

"Mom? Are you still there?"

"Of course," she says indignantly. "I wouldn't hang up on *you*." Ah, yes, there it is...my mother is back.

"Why is Dad home already?" I repeat the question. My mother ignores me again and starts chattering excitedly to someone in the background. I assume it's my father. I hear snippets of the conversation, *baby, Grandpa, Pop Pop…*

There is a shout of joy—presumably from my father. I kind of expected *that. He* didn't sob inconsolably and tell me I was ruining my life when I told him I got married. Although he did sneak behind the garage and chain smoke when he thought my mother wasn't looking.

"Mom!" I shout into the phone. "Why is Dad home at four o'clock in the afternoon?"

She finally comes back on the line and I can almost hear her trying to compose herself. I definitely can hear her move into another room, her clickity clacky heels. "Well, there was a little incident at work. It's no big deal—"

"What incident, Mom?" Worst case scenarios begin to fill my mind. He could have gotten hit by a car! Or stabbed! Or shot! *Oh my God! That's it! He got shot! He's lucky to be alive!* I am shaking and I have to sit down. *How could she not tell me he got shot at work?*

Stony silence continues to fill my ear.

"Mom!"

"It's really nothing…"

"If it's nothing then it'll be no big deal to tell me."

I hear her sigh dramatically and then she says, "You have to promise not to say anything to Beth or Joey."

Whoa! A Secret? *That Beth and Joey don't know? This is great! I am never the first person to learn a* Secret.

"Yeah, of course." It will kill me not to rub it in Beth's face that I know something she doesn't know, though.

Giant sigh again and Mom speaks. "He got suspended. Last week."

"What?" *My father, the most morally sound human being I've ever met in my life...got suspended?* "What happened?"

"He crashed the police car."

"Um, okay?" While I'm sure police car crashing is not optimal, I hardly think it's grounds for a *suspension.* "Why would they suspend him for that?"

"He was um...*under the influence.*" She's practically whispering.

I shake my head, trying to wrap my brain around this. *Under the influence? Of what?*

My dad doesn't drink. He doesn't even participate in toasts at weddings—he just pretends to sip the champagne. And then he pushes his glass toward my mother, who drinks enough for the both of them.

Could she mean...pills? *Drugs*? But that's impossible, too. Dad won't even take an ibuprofen for a headache. He could have a stake driven through his forehead and he would tell us he's fine. He's one of the original tough guys.

"What are you talking about, Mom? Under the influence of *what*?"

"Laughing gas." She says this so matter-of-factly that I'm certain she is trying to make a joke. Then I remember that my mother can't tell a joke to save her life. That's my dad's department with his corny dad jokes.

"Laughing gas? Where did he get laughing gas, Mom?"

"The dentist, Amy! What do you think, we have laughing gas sitting around in the medicine cabinet?" She sounds thoroughly annoyed with me, in turn making *me* annoyed at *her.*

I promise myself right then and there that I will be much more patient with my child. I cover my belly with my hand as I make that promise. I also silently swear that I will never be snarky with him, either.

"But why did the dentist give Dad laughing gas?" I feel like I'm trying to put together a jigsaw puzzle when important pieces gotten eaten by the family dog.

"Because he was having dental work, Amy!" Mom huffs as she speaks. She has definitely retreated into her default *I can't believe I gave birth to you, Amy* mode.

"Wait. He had dental work done...with laughing gas, and then got in his detective car? Why didn't you drive him home?"

"Because the stubborn old man never even told me he was *having* dental work done. He thought he could go back to work after having wisdom teeth removed."

Yup. That sounds like my dad.

"So he crashed the car because he had laughing gas?"

"Well, that and the bee."

"I'm sorry, it sounded like you said the *bee*?"

"A bee got up his sleeve. He's highly allergic, Amy."

"Yes, I know that, Mom."

"He was reaching for his Epipen—"

"And he crashed the car?"

"Into a hearse."

Once again, I think I am hearing things. *Is hearing loss a side effect of pregnancy?* I will have to ask on the Baby Days forum.

"A hearse? Like a funeral car?"

"Correct."

I drop my face into my hands. I don't even have any words.

"It was the funeral of the retired fire department chief," Mom volunteers. "Your father was apparently incoherent when he got out of the car. He had gotten stung by the bee. His face was swollen up. The Epipen was in his hand. Nobody knew what it was. They thought he was shooting up or something."

"Oh boy."

"It was a big mess. They're in the process of sorting everything out. With the dentist and why he was on the laughing gas and the bee up his sleeve and the Epipen in his hand."

"So he's not in trouble?"

"Well the suspension is only until they sort the whole thing out. He obviously wasn't under the influence of *illegal* substances."

"He still shouldn't have been driving."

"I know that, Amy. Your father is a stubborn man." She lowers her voice. "He's been very annoying since he's been home. Follows me everywhere. He's so bored. I can't watch any of my programs without him interrupting and asking a million questions."

"How does Joey not notice Dad has been home?"

More silence.

"Mom?"

"Well Joey's been sleeping all day."

What a surprise.

"Did she get a new job at night?"

"Not exactly. Well, sort of…"

"Did she or didn't she?" I really have to pee. I am ready to be done with this exhausting conversation with my mother.

"She's been staying up all night to take pictures of the stars and the sunrise."

"Huh?"

"It's for a new project. Something about a time lapse video. For the internet."

"Who the heck is going to look at a time lapse video of the sunrise on the internet?"

"I have no idea, Amy. I just know that your sister has this wonderful idea and you always have to mock her. Why do you do that?"

And...here we go again.

"I have to go, Mom. Tell Beth and Joey about the baby! Bye!" I hang up the phone before she can protest.

I shake my head and head to the bathroom to pee.

"Don't be like those crazy people," I tell my belly. "Be nice and normal when you come out."

And then I realize,

Crap, this baby is going to be related to a bunch of crazy people.

4.5

Maxwell Mommy: *I didn't use the cinnamon bun idea, but I told my husband finally. And my mom.*

Bun in the Oven: *Yikes. Telling mom's is hard.*

In a Baby Daze: *Moms, not mom's.*

Maxwell Mommy: *Telling my sister was actually worse. She makes everything I do sound like it's the biggest mistake.*

George's Gal: *I'm sorry, Maxwell Mommy. My SIL and MIL are like that.*

Eating 4 2: *Speaking of cinnamon buns, has anyone experienced a rapid weight gain since the nausea went away?*

She's Having My Baby: *Yes, I've been eating like a pig since my wife told me she's pregnant. Hahaha.*

In a Baby Daze: *Funny, She's Having My Baby.*

George's Gal: Oh my God yes! I feel like I could eat a horse now!

Eating 4 2: *Me too! I ate an entire box of Devil Dogs last night. That was AFTER the pint of Ben and Jerry's!*

Mom of 3: *Be careful of rapid weight gain! It could be a sign of something serious!*

Bun in the Oven: *Are you serious? Should I call my doctor? Or can it wait until my next appointment?*

Mom of 3: *No! Don't wait for your next appointment! Always call your doctor whenever you have any questions* *about your pregnancy. Trust me. I've done this three times already.*

****

I'm staring at the back wall of the doctor's exam room while he glides the wand over my abdomen. He's pushing a little too hard for my liking—and the fact that I wasn't allowed to pee before the exam is not helping matters. I feel like pee is about to leak out all over the table. So I'm distracting myself by looking at the pictures on the wall.

The diagrams in the pictures are nothing short of terrifying—different stages of birth. I am feeling like I may be violently ill as I wonder how it is humanly possible that a pelvic bone can accommodate a head the size of a cantaloupe. I start to wish that I had given more thought to this situation before I got myself into it.

Of course, that's exactly what my sister Beth said. Not that she had actually *said* that, but she certainly implied it when she called the other day.

I was not surprised when the phone had rung shortly after I hung up with my mother. Obviously, Mom had told her about the baby and she didn't waste any time calling me. I was stupid enough to think that she was calling to congratulate me and Roger. Ha! I should have known she would never work off *that* script. Beth's script went something like this:

Me: (picking up the phone) Hello?
Beth: (throat clearing, high pitched, nasal voice) Amy!

Me: (trying not to groan and be a polite adult) Hi, Beth. How are you?

Beth: (titters) The question isn't how *I'm* doing, is it? It should be how you're doing.

Me: Mom called you, huh?

Beth: Yes. My phone must have been busy when you tried to call me to tell me. I've been very busy with the new high profile case we've been building. And the wedding, of course. Derek's mother was absolutely apoplectic about the flowers we chose for the hall. What a debacle,I tell you.

(While this sounds like an unnatural response, I assure you, this is typical Beth. Each statement that comes out of her mouth must have a passive aggressive jab, somehow turn the conversation around to her, and use at least one big word that she knows I won't understand.)

Me: Sounds...busy. (I don't know any big words)

Beth: Yes. But you sound like you've been busy as well. (laughs) You are due way after the wedding, right? You're not going to need additional fittings to accommodate your...*girth* in February, are you?

(Beth and Derek are getting married in February. On Valentine's Day. How very cliché and nauseating of them.)

Me: I'll be fine by February, Beth (make mental note to ask Baby Days forum how long it takes to lose baby weight)

Beth: Oh, wonderful. I have to say, it is brave of you to bring a child into this world at such a young age. Derek and I are too selfish to give up all our free time and alone time in our twenties. We don't plan on procreating until we've done everything we want to do. And research has indicated that twenty-eight is the optimal age for a woman to give birth.

Me: (sautéing the beef for beef stir fry) Um, hmm.

Beth: But good for you, Amy. You don't care *what* people think of you. I would personally be completely aghast at the mere suggestion that I would have to give up everything and be a mother before I was ready.

(And on, and on, and on until I blessedly burnt dinner and the smoke detector went off, forcing me to end the conversation.)

"Well Mr. and Mrs. Maxwell, everything is looking perfect. The baby is measuring a little over eighteen weeks, as it should, and the heart looks normal as well."

Dr. Babin's voice brings me back to the present where I am naked from the waist down on a gurney with a bladder that may literally explode if I so much as cough.

Dr. Babin yanks off his gloves and rubs his hands together like he's actually going to dive in and deliver the baby right this moment. I sit up on the cot lined with the stupid crinkly paper, congratulating myself for having managed to contain all my pee inside my body during the process.

"So what now?" Roger asks. I am hoping Dr. Babin says *Now it's time for Amy to visit the bathroom!* But no.

"Now you can feel free to let your friends know about the baby! And prepare for the baby. Go shopping! Make a registry list! All those things new parents love to do. Everything is going swimmingly."

Roger turns green at the mere mention of shopping—he reaches in my purse where I keep the antacids. I get excited at the mention of shopping.

I know I shouldn't, being almost broke and all, but Roger got some good news a few days ago. Remember Robby Palmer, the moron who got the principal job? Yeah, well apparently he made vacation plans to spend the *whole* summer in Tahiti and isn't available to take the principal job until September. Instead of teaching summer school for peanuts, the board begged Roger to take over the principal position for the summer school. They doubled his salary to entice him. Little did they know, Roger probably would have done it for mere peanuts. At any rate, it alleviates our money troubles...*slightly*.

"You got your prenatal vitamins, correct?"

I nod. "Yes. At my initial appointment." I wince, waiting for Roger to get upset that I have kept the baby a secret from him for almost four months. Except he's too busy digging in my purse for antacids to even hear me.

"The nurse will make your next appointment when you stop at the desk. I'd like to see you in four weeks."

"Um, okay, sure." I start to sweat and my heart begins to race. I think I even leak a little pee. *I really have to pee.*

Dr. Babin misreads my facial expression for concern. For once, the only concern I have is when I can go to the bathroom. He pats my leg.

"If you have any questions, you can always call and speak to either me or my nurse, okay? Everything is going to be good. You guys just need to relax."

You don't want me to relax, Dr. Babin. I will pee on this table if I do.

Roger makes a strangled noise. I think he's trying to say, *Easy for you to say*, but I can't make it out because it sounds like someone is standing on his vocal cords.

"Oh, and do you want to know the sex?"

"The sex?" Roger squeaks out, turning purple.

"Yes, of the *baby*," Dr. Babin says, raising his bushy eyebrows at my husband's reaction.

"Oh, oh the baby," Roger stammers. "You can do that this early?"

Dr. Babin nods his head. "Yes. Sometimes the baby makes it difficult, but your baby was cooperative. I can tell you the sex with about 99% certainty in this case."

"Oh well, yeah. Of course," Roger babbles.

This is where I interject.

"Wait. We didn't discuss this! Maybe *I* don't want to know the sex of the baby. Maybe I want it to be a surprise!"

"Okay then," Roger stammers. He is sweating profusely. "Whatever you want, dear." He pops another antacid.

"You might as well record your voice saying that to her," Dr. Babin jokes. "It'll be your mantra for the next few months. Anything Amy wants, Amy gets. She is growing a human, after all."

That statement causes Roger to turn white as a sheet. He's like those color changing horses in *The Wizard of Oz* today.

"I *do* want to know," I announce. Although, I don't really even need anyone to tell me what I'm having. I know I'm having a boy. I *have* to be having a boy. I grew up with two sisters. I know what girls are like. I do *not* want to live with another female for the rest of my life. There is no way that God would torture me and give me a girl.

"The sex of the baby?" Dr. Babin whirls around to peer at me.

"I thought that's what we were talking about?" I feel oddly annoyed at him. Though I feel oddly annoyed at everything right now because I have to pee.

"Of course!" Dr. Babin flips open the chart and examines the ultrasound pictures. "Do you *really* want to know?"

I want to punch this little old man right now.

We nod and Dr. Babin grins.

"Congratulations Mr. and Mrs. Maxwell. You're having a...*girl*!"

"Oh my God," Roger mumbles. "Oh my God," he repeats, dropping his head in his hands.

Crap. We're having a girl.

5

July

You are 5 months pregnant. Your baby is the length of a small banana. Hair is starting to grow all over your baby—this downy hair is called lanugo—but don't worry, your baby won't be born looking like Bigfoot. This hair will be gone before the baby is born if the baby is born at full term (talk to your doctor about risk factors for premature birth!).

You may start to feel your baby move at this stage...it's called quickening and it sometimes feels like butterflies in your stomach. It can be alarming at first, but it's all normal and you will get used to it. (And you'll probably wish for these subtle movements later on in your pregnancy when it feels like your baby is using your bladder as a trampoline and your rib cage as a soccer goal.)

Speaking of soccer...be sure to include low impact exercise like walking into your routine and stay away from fatty and high caloric foods with little nutritional value. You don't want to put on more than 25-30 pounds when pregnant. Remember, the weight you put on, you have to take off at some point!

****

"This is where we keep the animals that have tags. We run the tags and try to contact the owners." Amanda is droning on in a bored sort of voice as she takes me through the shelter.

I have to pull the top of my T-shirt over my nose—the smell is horrendous. Even though my stomach has settled down over the last month or so (except for the heartburn—what is *that* about?), the most ridiculous things can send me running to the bathroom. My stomach flutters from the smell. I cover it with my hand, as if to silence it, even though I don't think there was any noise. Either I'm really hungry or I really am going to puke.

Amanda looks at me oddly. Actually, I've worked with Amanda for two weeks now—we spent most of that time painstakingly going over paperwork that needs to be filled out when an animal is brought into the shelter—and I don't think she has ever *not* looked odd. Oh, except when *Troy* comes in.

Troy is the "dog catcher". Well, actually Amanda corrected me when I called him that, informing me that Troy is an *animal control officer*. This is what happens when Troy comes in.

Amanda: Hi, Troy! (high pitched giggle, leans on a stack of papers on the counter, flutters her lashes)
Troy: (completely distracted by the snarling, partially-muzzled, possibly rabid dog that he is leading in through the front of the building) Um, yeah, hi.
Amanda: (leaning further across the counter, making her boobs pop out of the top of her very low cut shirt that she

shouldn't be wearing to work in the first place) Whatcha doing?

Troy: (as he continues to lead the dog into the back of the shelter, carefully keeping away from its angry jaws as it lunges toward his pant leg, not even glancing Amanda's way) Uh, huh.

Amanda: (giggling like an idiot...elbow sliding so far off on the stack of papers that her arm slips and she hits her face on the counter) "Ouch!"

Troy: (completely ignoring her as he enters the back room where the animal cages are kept) Let Bridget know I got one that needs to be seen by the vet.

Every. Damn. Time.

Wait. I might be wrong. I think he once asked her what time the deli down the block opened. You would have thought he asked her out for a steak dinner the way she carried on after he left, fluffing her hair and giggling to herself. Shesh.

Today she is *finally* letting me into the back room where the cages are kept. When I asked her about it the first day, she acted like it was a golden room where I had to earn access to. She made a point to say they didn't just let "anyone" back there.

I am not sure why they're hiding this room from the public. Maybe they think someone is going to take the dogs...but isn't that the point? Maybe it's because of how smelly it is. I mean, I like animals, but *yikes*.

We come to the cage where the puppy I brought in is being kept. She's sleeping, curled up like a ball of fluff. She pops to life when she hears us, running over to the side of the cage, whimpers and pawing at the bars. I swear she looks like she's begging me to take her out of there with her sad brown eyes.

I lean down and squeeze my hand between the bars to stroke her head. "Awww, she's still here?" It's been well over a month.

"Yes, Amy," Amanda says with a sigh. "I told you that we have a twenty-eight day waiting period for animals that are found. To make sure their owner doesn't show up looking for them."

"Oh, yeah, I remember." I nod. "But still, that was a while ago. I thought she would be adopted by now." I feel a stab of guilt that the puppy has been here this long. Maybe I should have tried to locate her owner on my own.

"Well, she won't be here for much longer. There's a family come in later to see her."

"Oh. Well, that's good."

"Actually, I think that might be them now," Amanda says, craning her neck to peek out the smoggy window. You would think someone would clean the windows around here every once in a while. I would mention it, but I don't really want that *someone* to be me. I don't do windows.

"Come on." Amanda pushes her way back into the lobby.

I hear doors slam and screechy voices reach the lobby before the family even makes their way inside.

"No! I wanna open the door!"

"You got to open the door last time!"

"That's not fair! I never get to open the door! Mooooooooooom! Tell him it's my turn to open the door!"

"You always get to press the elevator button! I never get to press the elevator button! That's not fair!"

"You pressed the elevator button yesterday!"

A harried looking mother pulls the door open. Her sunglasses are askew on the top of her head, her hair a tousled mess in a ponytail. There are dark circles and bags under her eyes. Three screaming boys between the ages of four and seven come tumbling into the lobby, followed by a tall and lanky man who I presume is their father.

He's staring at a cell phone and poking buttons, completely ignoring the scene of utter chaos unfolding in front of him. He puts the phone to his ear and starts speaking loudly to whoever is on the other end. The woman moves closer to the counter, shaking her head at his rudeness.

"Can I help you?" Amanda asks sweetly, in the voice that she usually reserves for interactions with Troy and no one else. I fold my hands and lean on the counter. This is interesting. I have yet to see her with a potential "customer". She must only be a bitch to people she works with. Well, actually, she must only be a bitch to me. She's nice to Bridget. Probably because Bridget is her boss and can fire her. I'm just a lowly peon.

"Yes," the woman says, yanking her purse from the crook of her elbow, where it has fallen, up to her shoulder. "We're here about the Australian Shepherd puppy?"

"Wonderful!" Amanda ducks below the counter and pops up with a clipboard. "I'll just need you to fill out the application, and then we'll have you meet the puppy."

"Of course," the mother says with a sigh as she takes the clipboard from Amanda's outstretched hand. Oblivious Dad is still talking on his cell phone.

"Absolutely!" he says in a booming voice. "We can meet at Victor's and go over the blueprints." He chuckles. "Oh yes. Definitely drinks."

"I want to meet the puppy now!" the oldest of the three boys screams, stomping his foot.

"Me, too!" one of his brothers insists. "Mama, I want to pet the puppy!"

"That's not fair!" the third kid protests. "If he gets to pet the puppy, I want to pet the puppy, too!"

"I have to fill this out guys, okay?" Harried Mom says as she plunks down on one of the plastic orange chairs in the lobby. "We have to do that first."

The kids continue to argue about who's going to pet the puppy as their mother fills out the application. They climb on the other chairs and one of the boys actually runs across her lap. She doesn't even appear to notice. The other two boys have fashioned guns from their fingers and are running around the lobby shouting "Phew, phew, phew!"

"You can't shoot me! You're dead! Lay on the ground! I shot you! Moooooom! Tell him he's dead!"

Harried Mom continues to ignore the kids as she scribbles on the application, while Oblivious Dad is still yelling into his phone. Something about S and P.

"Mooom!" The youngest kid starts poking at his mother's arm. He gets no response, so he moves on to his father who is standing in the corner. "Daaaaad!" He prods his father's legs and gets a totally different response.

The man's angry eyes burn a hole in the kid's skull. "What? Can't you see I'm busy?" He waves his hand toward Harried Mom. "Go bother your mother." He then spins on his heel and pushes open the door, stepping outside.

Meanwhile, the mother is handing the paperwork to Amanda and chuckling nervously. "The kids really want a puppy. It'll be good for them. Help them learn some responsibility." She sounds exactly like someone who is trying to convince herself of this fact.

"Sure thing," Amanda says, taking the application from her and pasting a fake smile on her face. "I'll take you to meet the puppy now, if you'd like." Amanda steps around the desk and heads toward the room with the cages.

"Yah!" The kids practically trample their mother and follow Amanda like the Pied Piper of Hamelin.

"Ewww! It smells!"

"Like farts!"

"You said farts!"

Hysterical laughter.

"Farts, farts, farts!"

Harried Mom is looking back at the front door, probably waiting for Oblivious Dad to return. Finally, she shrugs and follows the kids into the back room.

"And he's the one who wanted the dog for the kids," I hear her muttering to herself.

From the counter, I watch the mom and the kids through the glass partition. One of the boys climbs up the side of the cage, while the other two immediately make a beeline for the puppy.

As Amanda speaks to the mother, the oldest boy picks up the puppy and starts spinning in a circle with her. The brothers both start trying to grab at her. Within minutes, they are all wrestling on the floor, trying to get the puppy away from their brother. I suck in my breath, certain that the puppy is going to get crushed. If not right now, soon after this demonic clan brings her home.

I can't let them take this puppy! She'll die living with these little monsters. And the mother and father won't do anything to stop it.

I gnaw at my cuticles, trying to come up with a plan to save this puppy from these horrible people. I'm so nervous that my belly is flipping again.

When Amanda returns with the mom and the kids she says, "My supervisor has to check the application before we can approve it, though. I'm sure you'll get a call from her in a day or two."

"Oh yes. Great," Harried Mom says, looking even more harried than she had when she arrived—if that was even humanly possible. The kids are ripping flyers off the bulletin board in the corner. "Well, my number is on the application."

She leaves the building, all three of her children in tow, whapping each other over the head with the flyers that used to hang on the bulletin board.

"Geez," Amanda sighs after they're gone. "If my kids acted like that, I'd send them to military school."

"I'd send them to live with my mother. They wouldn't know what hit them."

"I'd send them to live with my evil stepmother," Amanda comments wryly. Then she laughs. "Those kids *definitely* wouldn't know what hit them."

Are we bonding? Oh my God...I think we're bonding over our mutual dislike for these kids!

"I'd get my tubes tied if I had one like that. There's no way I'd have *three* like that," I add.

Amanda's face freezes mid-laugh. "You shouldn't joke about infertility."

Okay...we're not bonding anymore...

"Um, sorry, I didn't mean to—"

"All some people want is a child and they aren't so blessed with them."

Amanda eyes me evilly. My belly flips. I swear Amanda looks at my belly, but it must be my imagination. There's no way she could know I'm pregnant. I'm wearing an oversized shirt and I um, forgot to mention the fact that I was pregnant on my application.

Okay, okay. Maybe I shouldn't have skipped it. But what if they refused to hire me because of it? I know Carol said that was illegal, but maybe in some jobs it's not. Like, I can't change cat litter, and maybe that was the deciding factor between employment and no employment.

I really hope no one asks me to change cat litter. I don't actually want to change cat litter, come to think of it.

"Listen, Amanda, I—"

"I'm going on lunch. I'm going to the deli," Amanda tells me before I can even finish apologizing. My stomach growls at the mention of lunch—it's been a whole two hours since I've eaten. *Maybe I'll get some Twinkies from the vending machine in the break room.*

Amanda shoves the clipboard at me. "Submit this application to Bridget. Tell her the family visit was fine."

"Okay," I tell her, watching her stomp out the front door. "I didn't want anything from the deli, thank you," I say softly when I am sure she is gone.

And this is when my evil plan hatches.

****

"Hi, um, Mrs...." I check the application, "Daniels?"

"David! Leave your brother alone!"

"Hi, um, is this the Daniels residence?"

"Put the fire poker down, Drew!"

She doesn't even need to answer my question. It has to be Mrs. Daniels.

"So this is..." I quickly realize that I need to lie here, "...*Amanda* from the shelter."

"Yes! Damien! I *am* going to get your father! I am *not* kidding!"

Why would you ask for trouble and name your kid Damien? You might as well have 666 tattooed on the back of his head at birth.

"I just wanted to let you know that owner of the puppy came to claim her shortly after you left." I cringe, waiting for the woman to get mad or suspicious. I really hope she doesn't call Bridget up to investigate—I probably won't have a job after that. But there's no way I can let these people take that puppy.

"Oh thank God," she sighs audibly. "Thank you, thank you, *thank* you!"

"There are other dogs that you—"

She hangs up the phone, leaving me staring at it.

"Who was that?" Amanda snaps.

I jump, startled. I didn't even hear her come in.

"Um, Mrs. Daniels." Not a lie.

"What about?"

"She wanted to tell us that she changed her mind…they don't want the dog after all." Not a *total* lie. She didn't *sound* like she wanted the dog.

Amanda frowns as she tosses her bag on the counter.

"Great. The puppy only has a few more weeks before—" She stops talking and unwraps her sandwich.

"Before what?" I ask, almost certain I know what is coming.

"You know," Amanda says in between bites, food falling out of her mouth and onto the Daniels' paperwork.

"But she's only been here for a few weeks. And she's a puppy! Who doesn't want a puppy?"

Amanda shrugs. "She's got a slight limp and all that."

"You can't even notice the limp!" The animal control vet had said it was a birth defect—not caused by me *not* hitting her with the car.

"People that want a puppy don't want a defective one."

"She's not defective!"

I feel lightheaded and short of breath. There is no way I am going to be responsible for this puppy's demise. I have to do something!

"I'm adopting her."

"What?" Amanda stares at me, mayo pooling in the corner of her mouth.

"Yeah. I'm filling out an application and I'm going to bring her home." I say this with so much confidence that I nearly believe myself.

Amanda stares at me incredulously. "Why did you bring her in to begin with then?"

I wrack my brain to come up with a plausible lie. "I wanted to talk about it with my husband."

"For a month and *a half?*"

"He was uh, away on business."

Liar, liar, pants on fire.

Amanda shakes her head and shoves a clipboard at me. "Well, stop talking and fill out the application so I can process it." She scoffs loudly and dips a handful of French fries into ketchup. "Just more paperwork for me. You couldn't decide this before you brought her in, huh?"

I open my mouth to respond, except she's muttering under her breath and I realize she isn't actually talking to me.

With shaking hands, I take the clipboard with the application and fill it out. I take care to put "none" under the section where it asks for the ages and names of children in the household. The baby doesn't count until she's born, right? Besides, if I put age 0 or something, Amanda will know I'm pregnant.

When I finish, I hand it over to Amanda. She barely glances at it as she sticks it in a manila envelope and shoves it under the counter.

"Bridget has to approve it," she tells me as she opens her diet soda.

"Bridget has to approve what?" Bridget enters the building as stealthily as Amanda did moments before. Amanda turns crimson.

"Um, just an application—"

"I filled out an application to adopt that puppy I found." I grab the paperwork from the envelope and hold it out to Bridget, who promptly claps her hands.

"Excellent! I'm so happy that you two found each other!" She waves away the application. "Just file that, Amanda. Put my signature stamp on it."

"But don't you have to—" Amanda looks very uncomfortable.

"Nah, it's just a formality. Just stamp it." Then she beams at me. "Isn't your shift over for today?"

I glance at my watch. It's two o'clock. My shift today ends at one thirty. "Yes, yes it is."

"What are you waiting for? Go get the puppy!"

I think Amanda is going to explode with indignation as she watches me enter the back room. I sidle up to the puppy's cage, lifting the latch. She was dozing when I entered, but as I open the gate, she pops up on her feet and squeaks that adorable little puppy squeak. She cocks her head to the side as if to ask *what are you doing*?

"Come on little Missy. You're coming home with me."

As if she understands my words, the little furball dives headfirst into my open arms. She nuzzles my chest and gazes up at me, love bursting from her eyes.

Crap. I'm bringing home a puppy and I promised Roger I wouldn't.

5.5

George's Gal: *I think I felt the baby move today!*

Bun in the Oven: *Congrats!*

Mum 2B: *I don't think I've felt it yet. What does it feel like?*

Mom of 3: *It's like a little fluttery feeling at first. It's hard to recognize with your first, but then you feel it much sooner with your next kiddos.*

Bun in the Oven: *Oh! I think I've been feeling that. Like butterflies?*

Mom of 3: *Exactly!*

Mum 2B: *I don't think I've felt anything like that yet…*

In a Baby Daze: *If you pay attention to your body you'll feel it. It's really not that difficult.*

She's Having My Baby: *I can't wait until I can feel the baby move. Right now my wife says he's moving but I can't feel it.*

Mom of 3: *Be patient. We'll all feel the babies move soon enough.*

Mum 2B: *Well, chance are I have felt it. Not that I would remember. Anyone else forgetting everything lately?*

Maxwell Mommy: *Oh yes! Definitely! I got a puppy and I forgot that my husband told me I shouldn't bring animals home from my job!*

Bun in the Oven: *Lol! I hope you blamed it on preggo brain!*

Eating 4 2: *Preggo brain is a real thing! I've had it with both of my pregnancies! I almost left my two year old at pre-school yesterday! I forgot where I dropped her off.*

In a Baby Daze: *Great. And you're allowed to procreate again.*

****

"Amy!" Carol rushes out from behind the counter, enveloping me in a giant hug. "Oh my, how I've missed you!"

"I've only been gone a few weeks, Carol!"

As she hugs me, I peek over her shoulder at the area behind the counter. It is one giant mess. There are shipping boxes everywhere and rolls of packing tape unraveled.

There is also a tray of Carol's homemade crumb cake on the counter. My stomach rumbles and flops again—I didn't have lunch and crumb cake is a perfectly acceptable lunch for a pregnant woman.

"What's going on—" I start to ask, but the puppy begins winding her way around our legs, tangling us together.

"Well, what have we here?" Carol asks with a chuckle, crouching down as much as she can with her legs entwined in leash.

"Come on little missy," I coax the dog into standing still while I untangle the leash (while trying to stay upright—what once used to be an easy task is starting to become daunting. I can't wait until my belly is so huge I can't see my feet. I'm going to be a fabulous klutz then).

"Awww, Missy. What a great name," Carol says as she pets the top of the puppy's head, legs free from the leash restraint.

"Oh that's not her—" I start to say. *But why not? She doesn't have a name actually. Missy is just as good a name as any other.*

"She doesn't have a name?" Carol asks.

"I just got her today. From the shelter."

I launch into the tale of how I almost ran the puppy over in the parking lot, and how it resulted in me getting a job at the animal shelter. And then how the future animal torturers came into the shelter and I sabotaged their adoption. Carol is laughing so hard that she's clutching her sides by the time I finish my story.

"Oh, Amy. You're always getting into some adventure."

She offers me the tray of crumb cake and I greedily attack it.

"I don't mean to get into things," I reply, taking two pieces of crumb cake. Biting into one, I am quickly reminded of the many reasons I love Carol—her divine crumb cake being at the top of that list. "How's it going here?"

Carol sighs and plops into the chair in front of the counter usually reserved for customers waiting to pick up their prescriptions. I notice that the place is deserted. Not a good sign at two o'clock on a Saturday afternoon—that's when most people are rushing in to pick up prescriptions before the pharmacy closes for the weekend. "You want coffee?"

I open my mouth to answer and my stomach feels like I am dropping in an elevator. "Oh!" I gasp, grabbing my belly.

"What's the matter?" Carol leaps to her feet. "Are you hurt?"

I shake my head, crumb flying out of my mouth and landing on the floor. Oh no! *The crumb is the best part!*

"No, my belly just flip flopped." I hold up the piece of crumb cake. "This is the first thing I've eaten since breakfast, so I'm probably hungry."

Carol smiles knowingly at me. "Flip flopping like butterflies in your stomach?"

I nod. "Maybe I'm just nervous about the new job." *Or getting a puppy when Roger specifically said no.* I'm going to have to figure out a plan to tell him about the puppy. Thank goodness he's at a charity golf tournament this afternoon with his friends from work and won't be home till later.

Shaking her head and laughing, Carol touches my belly. "Nope. You're just feeling movement. The baby is moving."

My jaw drops and I lose another crumb. For a split second I wonder if I can just scrape some crumb off the top of the other pieces. "Really? That's what it feels like? I've been feeling that all day! I can't believe I didn't know what it was." *What kind of mother doesn't even recognize her baby moving?*

"It's hard to recognize at first," Carol says reassuringly.

"I just don't think I'm going to be any good at this motherhood thing. I feel like I'm one step behind all the time so far. I can't figure anything out about being pregnant, and then I feel like an idiot when someone points out the obvious to me."

"Congrats, kiddo. You're getting your first taste of motherhood. Being one step behind all the time."

"That can't be right. It's just me. I'm going to be terrible at this. I'm just too young. Beth is right." My lip is quivering and I bite down hard to prevent myself from crying.

Carol takes my hands. "It isn't just you. Every single mother worth her salt feels like that sometimes. In fact, most of the time. My kids are in their thirties and I still question whether I know what I'm doing or not. It's part of the job. And the fact that you question yourself means that you're doing a great job."

"I'm just terrified of making mistakes," I croak out, trying to hold the tears at bay.

"Listen, I'm going to tell you what I told my own daughter when she had her first baby. You have to have faith in your ability. You *will* make mistakes. It's completely inevitable. But at the same time, it will be amazing. And that's why she named her daughter Faith."

Her words make resistance to my quivering lip futile. I start crying. Carol starts crying. I hug her, she hugs me. Harry pokes around the counter and sees us. He shakes his head and storms off. I hear muttering about *damn women*.

Carol and I pull apart and I try to smile at her. The puppy has made herself at home in one of the boxes on the floor.

"Enough about me. How's it going here?" I wave my hand at all the boxes, hoping Carol will fill me in on why it looks like a yard sale in the usually neat and tidy pharmacy.

Carol's face falls. "Ugh. This." She sweeps her arm toward the mess as well. "We're packing things up, kiddo. The pharmacy will officially be out of business the first of the month."

"The first of the month? That's only a week away!"

Carol nods. "Ever since Wal-drugs opened, we've steadily lost customers. Everyone is transferring their prescriptions over there because their hours are more convenient for working folks." Carol shrugs. "They just don't care about the personal touch of a pharmacist who knows you anymore."

"Oh, Carol, I'm sorry. I really hoped you would be able to stay open."

My heart is breaking for them. They opened this business before I was born. They were the first minority business owners in town and really had to fight to get customers back in the seventies. But once people realized how knowledgeable Harry was about medications and how friendly Carol was, they all started coming to this wonderful pharmacy. My own family included.

Carol shrugs. "It's really okay. It was time for us to retire anyway. Harry was fighting me on it, but now he has no choice. We can spend more time with our grandchildren and not feel guilty about not being here."

"Still, I'm sure it's difficult." I reach for another piece of crumb cake, so hungry that I don't care if I look like a pig or not.

"It will be. But at least we don't have to worry about more packages being stolen."

I cock my head to the side. "What? You had more packages stolen?"

Carol shakes her head. "Not us, but many of the other stores around here. We were at the monthly Business Owners meeting they hold downtown, and we found out that many of the small businesses in the area have still been losing packages. It's happened when kids are at school, too, so they don't think it's kids anymore. But the police say there's nothing they can do."

"That's terrible! And there's *nothing* they can do?"

Carol shrugs indifferently. "If there is, they're not looking for it."

"I'm sorry," I tell her.

"What are you sorry for? Are you stealing the packages?"

I turn bright red at the suggestion that I might do something remotely illegal. "No, of course not," I stammer.

"I'm just kidding, Amy," Carol says with a playful shrug. "Don't tell me you've lost your sense of humor already?"

"Already?"

Carol laughs a big, giant belly laughs that shakes her whole body. "Just wait." She points to my belly. "Once this kid is out, you may lose your sense of humor for a while."

I scrunch up my nose. "But why?"

"It's kind of hard to find things funny at two o'clock in the morning when you're half asleep changing a baby's diaper and they suddenly have projectile diarrhea all over your hair."

My jaw drops. "Wait, what? They can do that?"

Carol laughs again...this time for a full two minutes. "You'll be *amazed* at what they can do," she says when she finally catches her breath. She pats my arm sympathetically.

"Yikes," I groan, dropping my head in my hands. "Now I'm really nervous. This is going to be a long nine months."

"Amy, it's going to be a long eighteen *years*," Carol says.

I groan again, head still in my hands. "How am I going to do this?"

"The same way we all did it. With a little patience, a sense of humor, and occasional wine. Besides, your mother's raised three kids. Make sure you ask her for help when you need it."

Now it's my turn to laugh. "Carol, you know how it is with my mother. I never do anything right as far as she's concerned. I don't think I even would want her help."

"You know you can always call me too if you need something." Carol ducks behind the counter. She first grabs a sticky note off the counter and then a pen. Scribbling on the note, she tells me that she has gotten a cell phone...in case her daughter needs to get in contact with her quickly. Now that they are closing the pharmacy, they'll be traveling more and not available all the time.

"Thanks," I say, taking the note from her outstretched hand. I briefly consider that I should get a cell phone as well—in case I go into labor and I'm not by a phone. Roger already has one, but I didn't think that I really needed one when he got his. Now that *Carol* has a cell phone, I'm rethinking that. I'm usually a step ahead of her, technology wise.

Carol hugs me again. "It was wonderful seeing you, Amy. And you too little Missy." She reaches down to scratch the sleeping puppy behind the ears. Suddenly awake, Missy enthusiastically leaps to her feet, lapping up the attention. "Seriously, call me any time. Even two o'clock in the morning. I'm not usually sleeping anyway." I can tell by the bags that are usually under her eyes that she's not even joking about this.

I leave the pharmacy with a mixture of emotions—I'm happy that Carol is getting to retire, but I wish it wasn't under these conditions. Plus, the idea that someone or *someones* are going around town and stealing from the stores that I love to shop at...well, that's upsetting and infuriating. I wish the police would take it more seriously and try to figure out who is behind it instead of declaring that they can't do anything about it.

I am still contemplating this when I reach the door of our apartment building. Ignoring the bright sticker on the door that announces that no dogs are allowed, I pull the lobby door open and climb the three flights to our floor. There's no point in trying the elevator. It never works anyway.

When we get into the apartment, I let the puppy off the leash. She takes that as a signal to dash back and forth across the tile floor in the kitchen. I cringe listening to her tiny nails skittering back and forth, thankful that our downstairs neighbors work weekends and won't be home till much later on tonight.

Missy finally stops running and stares up at me with those puppy dog eyes that roped me in to begin with. She's panting. She probably needs water.

Crap! I didn't get her any bowls or food while I was out.

I open up the cabinets, looking for something I can put water in. I grab an empty plastic Chinese food container and fill it with water. I rummage through the other cabinets, looking for something to feed her. I could run to the store quickly, but I'm not sure I want to leave her alone just yet. Puppies are destructive aren't they? It's going to be a hard sell to Roger as it is—imagine how difficult it'll be if the puppy eats his shoes before I can even tell him we *have* a puppy?

I find a can of tuna in the back of the cabinet and stare at it for a minute. I bought a whole bunch of cans last week when they were on sale. Then I came home and one of the women on Baby Days website told me that tuna has mercury in it and that pregnant women aren't supposed to eat tuna. So now I have a dozen cans of tuna I can't eat.

"Cats like tuna, right?" I say to Missy, who is pawing at me. She cocks her head to the side, looking adorable. "I know you're not a cat, but you're an animal and this is all we have for your today. At least until Daddy gets home."

As I dump the tuna in another plastic container, my heart swells from calling Roger "Daddy". This puppy is going to be practice for us in a lot of ways.

The puppy stares at the tuna in the plastic container for a minute, and then she looks back up at me. And then she gobbles it up in one mouthful.

"Whoa, whoa!" I laugh. "Slow down! You'll get a belly ache!"

The puppy ignores me and finishes the tuna in less than a minute. She then trots off down the hall, presumably to explore her new space. I chase after her, not sure what she's going to do. She charges into the bedroom like she owns the place, and without any hesitation, she jumps up onto the bed, turns in a circle twice, and then plops down. She is fast asleep in seconds.

"Make yourself at home," I laugh, shaking my head. "You really do look comfortable," I say to the sleeping dog, yawning. Today has been mentally exhausting. I could probably use a nap myself. I kick off my shoes and curl up next to the dog.

The next thing I know, the front door is closing and I hear Roger calling out to me. "Amy?"

I jump to my feet, almost knocking the puppy off the bed. She doesn't seem to notice—she's in a deep sleep, probably dreaming sweet little puppy dreams of chasing sticks and cats.

"Amy?" Roger calls out again, this time his voice is louder. *Crap. The puppy! I have to tell him about the puppy before he finds her here sleeping on his pillow!*

"I'll be right there!" I call out, shoving my feet into my shoes and rushing out of the bedroom, closing the door behind me.

Roger is peeling off his sweat soaked polo shirt as he rifles through the mail on the kitchen table. His golf bag lays on the floor in the living room. My dad gave him his old set of clubs when he heard about this tournament. Roger was ecstatic. He loves to play golf, but clubs are expensive.

"Why is it so hot in here?" Roger complains, draping his shirt over the back of the chair.

I shrug. "I just got home. And then I fell asleep. It didn't feel hot to me then." But now I can feel the heat and I'm sweating buckets. That might also have something to do with the dog I smuggled into our apartment and I now have to tell him about.

Roger grumbles and stomps over to the AC unit in the living room, cranking the temperature down. We are lucky enough to have two—one in the living room and one in the bedroom, but it still gets really hot in our apartment in the summer. One of the drawbacks of living on the top floor of a four floor apartment building.

"How was golf?" I ask.

"Hot," he mumbles as he adjusts the levers on the AC unit. "Who has a golf tournament in July? So stupid."

He had been enthusiastic about it this morning. Maybe he didn't do so well. His friends all play regularly, so maybe it was embarrassing to be using your father-in-law's old clubs or something. Or maybe it really was just hot.

"What's for dinner?" he asks, standing in front of the unit and letting out an audible sigh of relief as the cold air blows on him.

"Oh, I haven't thought about it yet." I realize my stomach is growling as I step over to the freezer and peer inside. "Hot dogs?"

Roger makes a face. "I guess it'll have to do." Roger loves hot dogs, but this is the third time in two weeks we've eaten hot dogs. Just wait, the Baby Days ladies will tell me I'm not supposed to be eating hot dogs before long, and I can go into a full-fledged panic attack about eating so many hot dogs.

"And I can make some coleslaw," I say as I fish around in the fridge and find a bag of shredded cabbage that I had bought to make coleslaw for my parents' Father's Day BBQ but then proceeded to completely forget to make said coleslaw. I open the bag and sniff. It smells okay for being in the fridge for a month.

I am gathering the mayo for the coleslaw when I hear a high pitched scream. For a second I think that Mrs. Astor, the cranky old lady who lives next door to our apartment, is being murdered. Then I realize that it's Roger screaming. And that he's screaming from the bedroom.

Oh no! I forgot the puppy was in there!

"Um, Roger…" I drop the ingredients on the counter and rush to the bedroom where Roger is pinned up against the wall as the puppy leaps at him in a friendly, puppy way.

"What is this?" he yells, looking terrified.

I bend down and scoop up the puppy. "This is Missy. She's the puppy I rescued. Remember I told you about her? How I almost hit her with the car? And then I took her to the shelter?"

Roger's shoulders slump. "I also recall I told you not to bring animals home. You know I hate animals. Why isn't the puppy at the shelter?"

The puppy licks my face. "How can you hate animals? Who hates animals?"

"I do!" Roger violently unzips his dress pants and pulls them off. He tosses his pants onto the bed.

"Well you can't hate Missy," I say, holding out the puppy to Roger. His arms remain flaccid at his sides as Missy covers his face with puppy kisses. "Amy, I don't—" I can see my big tough husband melting before my very eyes. He can't resist this sweet puppy.

"Missy is going to be our practice child."

Roger grumbles, but allows Missy to continue to lick his face. He's putty in her hands. Well, putty in her paws anyway.

"I don't like the name Missy," Roger mutters as he reluctantly pets her head.

"Well," I say, eager to hasten his softening. "You can name her if you want."

Roger frowns, giving my proposal some thought. "Um, how about...Misty?"

I resist the urge to roll my eyes. Misty is not *any* different than Missy. It's practically the same name.

"Sure, Roger," I say, placing her on the floor. "Misty it is."

Missy, renamed Misty, settles herself down on Roger's foot. "Don't get too comfortable," he tells her. "You're not staying in this apartment long."

"What?" I am now confused. I thought we were keeping the puppy.

"We can't have animals here, Amy. Didn't you read the big sign on the front door?"

"Um, what sign?" I feign innocence.

Roger rolls his eyes. He knows I saw the sign. "We're going to have to move, Amy. This apartment is barely big enough for *us*, let alone us *plus* a baby *and* a dog."

"Into another apartment?" The puppy starts attacking Roger's bare legs. "No, Misty, no." I scold her and she stares up at me like I'm speaking a foreign language. Which, I guess I am. Poor dog thought her name was Missy.

Roger shakes his head. "No, I think it's time that we look into buying our own house."

Now I stare at Roger like he's the one speaking a foreign language. "Buy our own house? I thought you said there's no way we can afford that." I don't bring up the fact that not an entire month ago Roger was lamenting about the cost of a baby. I know the summer school principal job is more money than his teaching position, but it can't be *that* much more, can it?

"I was talking to Bruce Thompson—"

I resist the urge to groan. Bruce Thompson is one of the other teachers in the History department. He has three beach houses, a time share in Hawaii, and a boat. He never fails to remind Roger that he's doing it all wrong.

"And what did the great Bruce Thompson have to say?"

"Not much, but he did get me thinking. Renting is a waste of money. So…I've been doing some figuring," he tells me, pulling me closer.

Missy, er, Misty does not like that and lets out a low growl. But then she gets distracted by a piece of dust floating through the air and goes off to chase it.

"It turns out it would actually be cheaper for us to buy right now instead of rent. We have a little bit of money saved."

"Where?" This is news to me. Does he have it hidden in the floorboards like a Russian spy?

"In a savings account," Roger says sheepishly.

"We have a *savings* account?"

Roger nods. "Um. Just a little one. I put all my savings bonds in it when they matured. There's about five thousand dollars in it."

I pull away from him. "Five *thousand* dollars? We have five thousand dollars I didn't know about? Why didn't you tell me this instead of letting me completely stress out over the fact that I thought we were broke."

"Well, we're not rich, either," Roger says nervously. "Don't go running up the credit card bills. It's only enough for a down payment.

"Roger, I'm not even considering running up credit card bills. We're living on hot dogs, pork and beans, and Ramen noodles right now because I thought we couldn't afford chicken." I don't mention that I don't really want to eat chicken either.

"We can afford chicken, but don't go buying filet mignon."

As if I'd buy filet mignon! I don't even know how to pick out a steak.

Roger wraps his arms around me and all my stress just melts away. I was so worried about the dog and Roger flipping out about money. And now he's telling me it's okay...and we can buy a house. Today has been the most bizarre day.

Then I realize,

Crap! We're going to have to go look for a house.

6

August

You are 6 months pregnant. Your baby is getting fat—he or she is about the size of a grapefruit. He or she has translucent skin. This means the skin is see through and your baby's veins and blood vessels are visible through the skin. Don't worry, your baby still has a lot of growth ahead of him or her.

At this stage, you're not too uncomfortable yet, you're feeling better, and you look pregnant. A lot of women say the sixth month is bliss, but it's not without its issues. Backaches are starting to plague you, along with leg cramps. You will have to urinate much more frequently than ever before. Heartburn may be an ever present thorn in your side (or chest)…and no, it doesn't mean your baby will have a lot of hair. That's an old wives' tale. You'll encounter many of them…the way you're carrying, what you crave, whether you break out in pimples or not. While they are fun, they don't mean anything about your baby's gender or health. The most important way to ensure a healthy baby is too get plenty of rest, eat healthy foods, and stay hydrated, especially in the summer months.

****

I'm mopping the floor in the vestibule when the phone rings and Bridget grabs it. "Animal Shelter." A few seconds later, she cups her hand over the phone and calls out, "Troy!"

Troy appears almost out of nowhere (well, the back by the cages), Amanda trailing after him, tongue hanging out of her head. Troy looks quite...perturbed. Perhaps it's Amanda's presence. It perturbs me, too.

"Phone for you. It's Rodney," Bridget says as she hands Troy the phone. Rodney is the other animal control officer. He only works part time—thank goodness. Rodney wholeheartedly creeps me out with his bony, shaking hands and his acne encrusted face. He's the type of guy you see wanted for homicide on *America's Most Wanted* and you say, *yup, I can imagine him doing that.*

Troy places his keys on the counter, looking sheepish as he takes the phone from Bridget's outstretched hand. "Uh, Troy here."

Rodney starts talking and pink creeps up Troy's neck. His eyes fall on Bridget—he turns around and speaks into the receiver in a hushed voice.

Bridget is busy with paperwork on the counter and doesn't seem to notice, but I watch Amanda gawk at him. It's ridiculous. He's not even that good looking. Alright, so he's a hunk, but he's a jerk with no personality. I don't get why she's so gaga over him.

"Okay," Troy says into the phone and reaches over the counter to hang it up.

"Everything okay?" Amanda asks, sprawling across the counter and pushing her boobs out of her shirt. Her sickeningly sweet voice should be poured over waffles.

"Yeah fine." Troy doesn't even look at her as he grabs his giant keyring from the counter. "Okay, well I'm going to go check out the squirrel situation on Tennyson then."

"Squirrel situation?" Bridget asks, raising her eyebrows.

"Yeah," Troy says, shuffling his feet. "That's why Rodney called. His neighbor, uh, has been complaining of squirrels. In the attic."

"We just drop off traps in squirrel situations, Troy," Bridget reminds him.

"Yeah, that's what I'm going to do." Troy has one hand on the front door. Amanda is sliding across the counter like he's a magnet, pulling her in. I want to vomit.

"Why doesn't Rodney come get the traps?" Bridget asks. Although, I know this would not be her preference. I saw her shudder the last time Rodney was in the same room with her.

"His, uh, car broke down." Troy says as he pushes the door open. Which is a bold-faced lie. Rodney rides a bike. A two wheeler, not a motorcycle.

"Don't you need to get the traps from the back?" Bridget asks, peering at him suspiciously.

"Um, no. I have them in my truck." He is standing in the open doorway, gazing out into the parking lot like he wants to bolt.

Before Bridget can ask him another question, the phone rings again and Bridget sighs. "Animal Control." Troy takes the opportunity to scram.

Bridget looks down at the counter as she's speaking on the phone. "Could you hold on a minute?" She covers the phone and hands me a sheet of paper. "Troy forgot the paperwork for the squirrel traps. Can you run this out to him before he leaves, Amy?"

I swear Amanda is like a turkey vulture on roadkill as she lunges for the paperwork. "I'll take it him!"

Bridget is too quick and pulls it away before Amanda can get her mitts on it. "Amy is halfway out the door. She can do it." She shakes the papers at me. "Go on, Amy. Quick, before he leaves."

After securing the mop in the bucket, I take the paperwork from Bridget's outstretched hand, feeling Amanda's hard gaze on the back of my neck. She may or may not be burning a hole in my skin—I can't tell and there is no way I'm turning around to look at her. She could incinerate me with that stare.

Keeping my head down, I push the door open and march out into the parking lot after Troy, thankful that no cars are pulling in. I would be flattened like a pancake at the speed people pull into this parking lot.

I head around the back of the building where Troy usually parks the van. The back of the van is open—Troy's khaki clad pants and steel-tipped boots are visible from the knee down.

"Troy!" I call out, waving the paperwork in the air.

Troy whirls around to face me, eyes wide, like a kid caught with his hand in the cookie jar. The back of the van is only open for the briefest second before Troy jumps out of the way and slams the door shut, but it is long enough for me to get a glimpse of the cages...and packages. *Lots* of packages.

"What?" Troy snaps, sweat beading on his forehead.

"Um, Bridget said you forgot this." I hold out the paperwork, hand trembling. I haven't had much contact with Troy (other than watching Amanda swoon in his presence), but at this moment, he terrifies me almost as much as Rodney does. Maybe it's because his biceps are the size of my thighs. And he looks really, *really* uncomfortable—like a cornered animal just before he bites the zookeeper's head off.

"Thanks," Troy says, snatching the papers from my hand. I guess I don't leave fast enough because he snarkily asks, "Do you *need* something?"

I shake my head and turn on my heel, speed walking to the front of the building. I hear a door slam, presumably Troy getting into the van. The engine roars to life and he speeds past me before I can even get inside, swerving as he approaches, nearly hitting me in the process. My hand goes to my midsection without even thinking. The baby flips in response. I wonder if she can sense my nervousness.

"Don't worry," I murmur. "I'll protect you."

"Was that Troy?"

Amanda has snuck up on me again.

"Geez, Amanda," I gasp, clutching my chest. "You scared me."

"Who were you talking to?" She eyes me suspiciously.

I drop my hands to my sides. I've been working at the shelter for over two months and I doubt that they would fire me if they found out I was pregnant, but Amanda is *not* the person I want discovering my secret.

"Nobody."

"You didn't answer my question," Amanda accuses.

I thought I did. I was talking to nobody.

"Was that Troy?"

"Oh, yeah."

She giggles in that stupid school girl way of hers. "Oh what a naughty guy. He better be careful peeling out of here.

Bridget won't like it if she sees that. I'll have to tell him later. When we go out for drinks." She narrows her eyes at me—I think she's trying to make herself look smug or something, but she only succeeds in looking like she's had a poop stuck up her butt for a week. "Yes, we're going out for drinks tonight," she repeats, in case I didn't hear her the first time she said it.

"Yes, I know. I was there when Troy invited everyone out for drinks for his birthday."

Amanda's smug face falls quickly. "Well, no one else is going. It's just going to be me and him. So it's like a date."

"Right." I couldn't care less if she goes on a date with Troy. Right now, I want to get out of the broiling hot sun. I usually love the heat of the summer, but for some reason, I seem to be getting overheated lately.

I push past her and grab the door handle. Entering the building, I am hit with not only a blast of cool air, but the stench of animals. For some reason, the smell makes my legs wobbly. I feel myself slipping on the floor that I just mopped, my legs flying out from underneath me. And the world goes black.

****

The next thing I know, I'm being loaded into a stretcher, Bridget's concerned face is peering down at me.

"Oh my gosh, Amy! You had me so worried!" She's chewing her nails. I blink my eyes and see a female paramedic next to me, fiddling with an IV. Behind her is Amanda...scowling as usual.

"What happened?" I feel groggy and my head is achy—not like I have a headache, but more like I hit it or something.

"You slipped in the vestibule and then you passed out," Bridget says.

"Ma'am, do you have any medical conditions that we should know about? Like diabetes or seizure history?" The paramedic has ceased playing with the IV bag and is now standing next to me with a clipboard in her hands.

Is pregnant considered a medical condition? I guess it's something that a medical professional should know about if they're trying to figure out what's wrong with me. Wait! Is something wrong with me? Am I dying? Is it normal for a pregnant woman to pass out? Oh my gosh, what if I am diabetic or something? I haven't gone for my glucose test yet, so I could be diabetic, right?

Suddenly I hear a rapid beeping noise.

"Ma'am. Your heart rate is spiking. Try to calm down a bit." A male paramedic is admonishing me as he stands next to the first paramedic, the one who is waiting for the answer to the question of whether or not I have a medical condition.

I glance uneasily at Bridget (and Amanda behind her) wondering if I'm about to get fired for not telling them that I'm pregnant. Still, if it comes down to the job or the baby, of course I'm going to choose the baby. Isn't that the right thing for a mother to do?

"I'm pregnant," I whisper to the paramedic.

She lowers her ear to my face. "I'm sorry, I couldn't hear you."

"I'm pregnant," I whisper again.

"Could you say that a little louder?" the paramedic asks. "I still can't hear you and I—"

"She said she's pregnant!" Amanda nearly shoves her out of the way to reach the side of the stretcher. "You neglected to tell *us* you were pregnant when you applied for the job, Amy." She crosses her arms over her chest, smugness replacing the hatred in her eyes.

"So what, Amanda. Maybe Amy didn't want to share her good news with us yet. You don't go blabbing to everyone that you're pregnant." Bridget moves Amanda out of the way and smiles down at me. "In fact, I didn't tell anyone I was pregnant with my first until I was almost seven months! I was so nervous I would mess up or that I was imagining being pregnant or something."

"But...what about the cats?" Amanda is stammering, shocked expression now replacing the smugness. Amanda's face is a medley of emotion today. "Pregnant women aren't supposed to change cat litter. That's supposed to be one of Amy's jobs."

Bridget waves her hand dismissively. "You can change the cat litter for her."

Oh great. As if Amanda didn't despise me before. Her eyes are tiny slits, shooting out laser beams of absolute hatred right now.

"Do you want us to take you to the hospital, ma'am? You've had a bag of IV fluids and your vitals are stable. You're not showing any signs of a seizure, so if you're feeling okay, you can go home. But if you still feel woozy, we can take you to the hospital for assessment." I look up at the male paramedic and see that the IV bag is empty. Which explains my sudden urge to pee like a racehorse.

"I can drive her home. Or to the hospital," Bridget says. "Now that I know she's just pregnant and isn't having a medical emergency."

"I got her!" I hear Roger's voice from somewhere, echoing on the cement walls of the vestibule.

"Roger?"

"I hope you don't mind, I pulled your file and called your husband. You had him listed as an emergency contact," Bridget tells me.

"Of course I don't mind. Thank you," I reply. Of course I want my husband with me if I have to go to the hospital. But when Roger's panic-stricken face emerges next to the stretcher, I realize that maybe I *don't* want him here.

"Are you okay, Amy?" He nearly smothers me with his arms as he reaches over the stretcher to hug me.

"She's fine. She just needed some fluids," the female paramedic tells him. "But she could probably use some breathing room, too."

"What happened?" Roger asks.

"I think I slipped and passed out. Or maybe passed out and slipped. I'm not sure," I tell him.

"You could be shaky from being dehydrated. That might be why you slipped," the male paramedic says. "That's why we gave you IV fluids."

"Or you could have just been an idiot who slipped on the wet floor," I hear Amanda mutter.

Roger relaxes his grip on me. "Didn't I tell you that you should be drinking more water?" He turns to the male paramedic. "I told her she should stop drinking so much ice tea and drink more water."

"Ice tea is bad for you when you're pregnant," Amanda admonishes. "You shouldn't be having caffeine."

"How would you know?" Bridget scoffs. "You don't have any kids."

"Well that's—" Amanda starts to speak, but Bridget interrupts her.

"Put out the wet floor sign, Amanda. So no one else slips."

Amanda transfers her evil look to Bridget, turns on her heel, and stomps off to the back to get the wet floor signs.

Bridget rolls her eyes at me and then turns her attention to Roger. "You sure you'll be okay? I can drive her and you can follow behind."

"Yeah," I say. "I want to go home. I'll be fine."

Roger puffs out his chest like a proud peacock. "Yes. We'll be fine." He takes my arm and helps me sit up. Not realizing that I am still hooked up to the IV, he continues to pull me off of the stretcher.

"Hold on a second, Roger!"

Too late. The IV is yanked out of my arm.

"Mr. Maxwell!" The female paramedic is grabbing gauze pads and pressing them against the crook of my arm to stop the bleeding.

"Sorry!" He holds up his hands and backs away from the stretcher.

"This is why husbands should be nowhere near pregnant wives," Bridget mutters under her breath. "I should know. I've been through three husbands while pregnant."

I recoil. Bridget looks like she is thirty years old. I can't imagine that she even *has* three kids, let alone has been married three times. She must sense my shock because she laughs.

"I got started young. Married right out of high school. Divorced two years later after baby number one. Then followed that pattern every two years. I'm still on the look-out for Mr. Right."

"Ah, okay." What are you supposed to say when your boss reveals a little tidbit like that to you?

"Maybe I should stop looking. I've had enough babies." She laughs. I guess this is supposed to be funny. I'm not sure. I feel so out of it that I'm not sure of anything right now. My head hurts, but I laugh anyway.

"You can take her home now, sir," the male paramedic says as he finishes taping the gauze pad to my arm with hospital tape. "Keep an eye out for signs of a concussion."

"Signs like what?" Roger asks with concern. "Maybe she should go to the hospital?"

"No, Roger, I'll be fine," I insist as the paramedic hands Roger a sheet with signs and symptoms of a concussion.

"Make sure she's drinking lots of fluids," the female paramedic adds. "She could go into premature labor if she gets dehydrated again."

"I can?" This is news to me. I *thought* I had been frightened about every possible scenario of what could go wrong by the fellow moms on the Baby Days website. Every time I turned the computer on I ended up fearing for my life and the baby's life. The other day I was certain I had killed the baby by eating a bagel with cream cheese and lox. I went on the website for some reassurance, but I didn't get much. Mom of 3 certainly thought I was worthy of being reported to

DYFS for my ignorance regarding soft cheeses and uncooked fish.

The female paramedic pats my arm. "It's not likely, but you need to take care of yourself and the baby in this heat."

Comforted by her words, I allow Roger to help me down off the stretcher (this time, no blood was shed) and walk me to the door.

"Feel better, Amy!" Bridget calls to my back. "Don't worry about coming in tomorrow if you don't feel well. I can get Amanda to cover your shift."

Thank goodness Amanda isn't within earshot or she would probably lynch me. "Thanks." And then I remember I forgot my purse in the break room. "My purse," I tell Roger. "I need to get it out of the break room."

"Okay." He continues to clutch my arm until I shake him off. "I'm fine by myself."

He looks crestfallen, and I feel bad, but the last thing I need is Roger hovering over me like a nursemaid of some kind. "I'll be right back." I offer him a peck on the cheek as a peace offering of sorts.

"I'll be right here!" He calls out to me as I head down the hallway. I push the door to the break room open to find Amanda and Troy sitting at the table, heads together, whispering feverishly. Their heads snap up when I walk into the room. Troy glowers at me—I didn't even realize he had come back to the shelter. *How long was I out for?*

"Um, just need to get my purse," I mumble and turn to my locker on the opposite wall. I feel their communal stare on my back. I quickly retrieve my purse and dash out of the room without looking at them again. The door makes a whooshing noise as it closes, but I can still hear Amanda's voice as I sling my purse over my shoulder.

"She's such a bitch."

Crap. They both hate me now.

6.5

Bun in the Oven: *My GOD is it hot lately.*

Mum 2B: *It's even hot in England. It's never hot here.*

In a Baby Daze: *It's summer. What do you expect?*

She's Having My Baby: *Even I'm hot. And I'm never hot.*

Eating 4 2: *Yes! It's so hot that I can barely eat. Well, that and the fact that I feel like I'm as big as a house and I can't see my feet. I don't think I have any room for food in my stomach because it's being squished by the baby.*

Bun in the Oven: *How are you all handling the heat? Our air conditioner unit broke and it's going to be a few days before my boyfriend can pick up a new one at the store. I've been standing in front of the open freezer door.*

George's Gal: *That's terrible Bun! I have working AC and I still find myself standing in front of it, trying to get cool.*

Maxwell Mommy: *We're having a heat wave where I live, too. I passed out at work!*

Mom of 3: *Don't stand in front of the air conditioner! Or the freezer! You shouldn't be putting your body through extreme temperature changes! And Maxwell Mommy, you need to drink more water. You must be dehydrated.*

Maxwell Mommy: *I think if I drink any more water, I'll never stop peeing.*

Bun in the Oven: *I know! I got up 5 times last night to pee!*

Mum 2B: *Me too!*

In a Baby Daze: *I got up 6 times.*

George's Gal: *I feel like I'm not getting enough sleep anymore because I'm getting up so much to pee!*
Mom of 3: *Wait till the baby comes. You'll never sleep again.*

****

My bladder issues are creating a common scene in our house:

Roger: (rapping feverishly at the bathroom door) Amy! Our appointment is in fifteen minutes! And it's across town!
Me: I'll be out in one minute. *Hold on*!
Roger: But how can you have to pee again? You just went ten minutes ago!
Me: Roger, I'll be there in a minute!
Roger: Hurry up! (paces in front of the bathroom door)
Me: You standing by the bathroom door isn't going to help me pee any faster!

I have to pee...everywhere I go. It annoys and frustrates Roger. He's become a little short with me. For some reason, my quickly expanding waistline has convinced him that we need to find a house like...yesterday. In the past two weeks, he's dragged me to a dozen open houses and set up appointments with three different realtors because he felt the first two weren't fast enough.

Today is our second day out with Eva, the third real estate agent. Eva has a thick Polish accent, making it difficult to understand her, but she showed up on time for the first appointment with us, so she's golden in Roger's eyes. That and the fact she wears very low cut blouses that show off her cleavage and tight skirts that accentuate her round and perky butt. Because having a real estate agent like that around is exactly what will make your pregnant wife feel good about herself.

I eventually finish peeing (for the moment) and we head out to meet the realtor. But not before securing Misty in her crate. I really didn't want to have to crate train her, but she literally tore apart the sofa and ate the stuffing the first time we left her alone. I thought Roger was going to keel over and die when he came home to *Stuffing-gedeon* in our living room. It seriously looked like a snowstorm had touched down inside the apartment. Misty got a crate the next day. She hates it.

We drive to the other side of town and cross over the railroad tracks into the next town. "Where are we going?" I ask Roger. "This is Dayville. I thought we were looking in our town. I'm not sure I want to live in Dayville."

Dayville is filled with older homes…and older people. It's nice, but there's never anything for sale there because the people in Dayville refuse to sell their houses. They don't like interlopers…since many of the people that live there were practically born in those houses.

Roger's eyes twinkle, but they don't leave the road. "Eva found a house that's not too far out of our price range. Much cheaper than the other houses in the area."

I eye him suspiciously. "What do you mean by *not too far out of our price range*?" Our price range is somewhere between Bohemian shack on a deserted island and homeless person refrigerator box.

"Don't worry about it, Amy," Roger says dismissively. "It's a deal too good to pass up."

"I *am* worried about it. Why is it cheaper?" I recall the movie *Money Pit* with Tom Hanks. That was a deal too good to pass up, too. I am envisioning collapsing staircases and falling through holes in the floor.

"Well the owners are really...um, dead."

I twist my body in the seat, which is not a small feat at six and a half months pregnant, and stare at him. "They weren't murdered in the house, were they?" I wrack my brain trying to recall if I ever heard of a murder in Dayville.

Roger laughs. "No, Amy. Your imagination is crazy."

"Well then how did they die?" I ask with an arched eyebrow.

"Don't know," Roger says. "Probably old age. They were old. I just know that they're not alive anymore and their daughter is very motivated to sell because she lives in California and wants to get on with her life. She's practically giving the house away."

"So you *don't* know that they weren't murdered in the house," I grumble as we pull up in front of an older two story home.

"Could you please not talk about murder when we see Eva?" Roger begs as he puts the car in park.

"I don't know if I want to live in Dayville. I've heard the neighbors don't like young people. And families."

Roger waves his hand in front of his face dismissively. "Please, those people can't live forever. You'll see. In ten years it'll be nothing *but* young people and families. And we'll be the first young family here."

I cross my arms over my chest. I guess he does have a point, but I'm feeling prickly and I don't want to agree with him just yet.

"It's eleven o'clock. Where is the *fabulous* Eva?" I ask, voice dripping with sarcasm as I stare out the window at the house. There's a shutter hanging off a window and the front yard looks overgrown with weeds, but for a house in Dayville that's allegedly in our budget...that isn't too bad. At least it isn't sinking into the ground like the last house we looked at.

Roger looks at his watch. I'm pretty sure he's annoyed that Eva is late, but he'll never say it. "Um, I'm sure she's just held up in traffic."

"There is no traffic in Dayville." I turn my head and start to say something snarky about how no traffic is *allowed* in Dayville, but something distracts me. I must have my mouth open because Roger asks me what I'm staring at.

I point to the van that is parked in front of the house next door.

"That's Troy's van. The guy that I work with at the Animal Shelter. I wonder why he's here in Dayville. Dayville has its own animal shelter."

"He probably lives here," Roger says as he pinks at lint on his pants and casually glances at his watch again.

"That's just great," I say just as I spy Troy coming around the back of the house with a large package in his arms, head swiveling left and right as he checks out his surroundings.

I duck down in the front seat, not wanting him to see me. It bears mentioning that this is also not an easy feat for someone six and a half months pregnant.

"Why are you hiding like that, Amy?" Roger peers down at me from the driver's seat.

"I don't want him to see me. He's not really a nice guy. He'll get mad if he sees me."

"Well, you're not doing him any harm by sitting in a parked car."

I don't mention to Roger that Troy attempted to run me over with the van parked in front of us a few weeks ago. And that Troy's murder attempt is probably the very thing that made me pass out. Well, that and the fact that I was totally dehydrated and slipped on the floor and I'm pregnant.

"Come on. Eva's here." Roger practically leaps from the vehicle to go greet his precious Eva. I lift my head and peer over the dashboard. Troy's van is gone.

Sighing with relief, I sit up and open the car door, stepping out of the car and smoothing out my sundress.

"Amy!" Eva squeals and trots over to me, arms flung open. Yes. She actually trots. I couldn't imagine that she could possibly do anything else in the six inch stilettos and teeny tiny blood-red wrap dress that she is wearing. She gathers me to her generously displayed bosom, squishing my face against it in the process.

"Hi," I mumble into her boobs.

"Wait till you see this house!" Eva gushes, waving her arms enthusiastically. "This is a…what's the word? Ah, *charmer* for sure. It is not going to last long at this price." She lowers her voice to a whisper and indicates that we should get closer. Roger does willingly. "I told you on the phone, Roggie, the owner is extremely motivated to sell. Wink, wink." She winks seductively, her never-ending eyelashes brushing the top of her cheek.

Roggie? What the hell kind of name is that?

"Gotcha," Roger replies, attempting to wink himself. Instead, he looks like he's having a stroke. I just roll my eyes and turn my attention to the house in front of me.

It is set back far from the road—and the street seems to be quiet as well—both bonuses in my book, especially with the baby coming and all. I rub my belly as I continue to gaze at the house. Roger practically runs toward it as I waddle up the front walkway with Eva.

"As you see, it needs some work, but the owners made it very nice inside. Until the poor dears went a nursing home last year." Roger turns and raises his eyebrow as if to say *See, they weren't murdered in the house.*

I ignore Roger and he rushes through the front door. I lean in closer to Eva.

"What can you tell me about the neighbor next door?" I whisper. I don't want Roger to know that I'm trying to gather some intel on Troy.

"Oh, it is a little old lady. Poor thing, all alone. No kids and no husband. She does not leave the house for anything. And she only has a home health aide come once a week. She has everything delivered to her...even her medicines."

I stare at her for a second. Troy is *definitely* not a little old lady, nor is he a home health aide. "Are you sure?" I ask, pointing to the house that I saw him emerge from earlier.

"I'm absolutely sure. I've been trying to get her to sell. You know, to go into a nursing home where someone will take care of her."

"Come look at this Amy!" Roger has managed not only to get into the house in the time it takes me to get up the front walk, but to rush up the staircase and hang out the top floor window. It's kind of like a castle. I think it's called a turret. I must admit, I *am* impressed.

Eva leads me into the house and up the staircase—the bottom step makes a creaking noise when I step on it, but it seems sturdy otherwise. There is an open area at the top of the stairs—five open doors branch off from this area. One I can tell is the bathroom and the other four look like bedrooms.

"He's in this room," Eva says, pointing to the open door at the end of the hall. We enter and discover there are three small steps to climb before entering the spacious room. This is a perfect room for a master bedroom. I can see Roger still hanging out the window as we approach.

"Hey! Come look at the view!" he calls to me.

I step over to the window and I have to admit, it *is* a nice view—much nicer than the view of the top of the dumpster that we currently have in our bedroom. I can see all the way up the street. My belly squeezes and I cross my legs so I don't pee my pants.

"Very nice. I have to pee," I announce.

Roger groans and covers his eyes with his palm. "You haven't even had anything to drink!"

I shrug. "I can't help it that my bladder is the size of a peanut, Roger."

"The bathroom is the first door on the left," Eva says, pointing toward the hallway. I thank her and scuttle from the room and toward the bathroom, leaving them to discuss the intricacies of the house.

The bathroom is in need of a good scrubbing, but the toilet flushes and the sink runs without leaking—I'm sure that will thrill Roger. The thing that doesn't thrill me is the window in the shower stall.

I step into the shower stall and push aside the plastic curtain. The window looks out into the neighbor's backyard—she's got a huge vegetable garden in the corner and lone folding chair on the porch. It's kind of sad.

Just as I go to turn away, I see the back door open and an elderly lady hobbles out with a cane. She pauses on the deck and scratches her head as she looks back and forth—like she's searching for something. Something...like a package.

****

"What did you think of the house?" Roger asks excitedly as I attempt to strap myself into the passenger seat. *Attempt* being the operative word here. Obviously seat belts were not designed with pregnant women in mind.

"It's uh, great," I reply. Before we left, Roger said he wanted to put an offer in on the house and I had told him okay without really thinking about it. To say my mind is elsewhere would be the understatement of the year. I have about a billion thoughts scrolling through the teleprompter of my mind.

What were those packages in the back of Troy's van? Were they stolen?

Is Troy responsible for the thefts from the businesses in town?

Is Troy stealing packages from the porches of little old ladies in Dayville?

What am I going to do about this?

Not once did I think, *Maybe I should call the police about this.* Nope. I blame this faulty thinking on pregnancy brain, of course.

I'm trying desperately to come up with a plan of action when I notice Roger is pulling into the parking lot of the hospital.

"What are you doing?" I ask with a wrinkled up brow. *Is he hurt or sick and I didn't notice? He's been babbling on since we left the old house, but I thought he was just excited about putting in an offer. You really need to pay attention, Amy.*

Roger looks at me with concern. "The class? Remember?"

The class? What—oh! The class!

Last week when I had gone for my appointment, Dr. Babin reminded me that I needed to sign up for a childbirth class. I panicked because I had forgotten all about that and I was afraid we wouldn't get into a class before my due date. Maria, who looks like she's going to burst at this point, told me she would get me into the childbirth class that she was running...today. I had forgotten all about it. Thank goodness Roger remembered it.

Roger shuts off the car and I groan as I unbuckle and heave myself out of the car. I have to pee again. I don't tell Roger. He's just going to complain about it. I guess I can hold it for a few minutes. Because it's such a major inconvenience for *him.*

We enter the hospital building and an attendant comes rushing at us with a wheelchair. "Labor and Delivery?" He looks panicked. He also looks about twelve years old. Maybe it's his first day.

"No, no," I say, waving my hand. "I'm not in labor."

"Oh." The boy appears crestfallen. It *must* be his first day.

"But I do need to get to the Atrium for a class. Can you tell us how to get there?"

He beams at me and points to the chair. "Hop in!"

I start to tell him that I don't need the chair, but I don't want to break his heart. Besides, I've been on my feet all day. I lower myself into the wheelchair and he speedily dashes us over to the elevator and up to the third floor where the Atrium is located.

"Here you are!" he says, chair screeching to a halt in front of an expansive conference room. The door is open and I can see a few pregnant women setting up pillows and blankets. I can also see a line of pregnant women snaking into the bathroom at the end of the hall.

"Oh, I forgot the pillows at home," I tell Roger, grabbing his arm.

"Do you want me to go home for them?"

"No need. We have plenty to go around." I hear Maria's voice and see her exiting the conference room. She points behind her. "On the table in the back."

"Where are you going?" I ask her as Roger pulls me out of the wheelchair.

"Little lasses room," she says with a twinkle in her eye. "There's no way I'm getting through a two hour class without it."

"Two hours?" Roger looks like he's going to lose his mind. "The real estate agent might be trying to get in touch with us!"

I place my hand on his arm. "She said it might be a few days until the owner's daughter gets back to her about the offer. Relax."

"But...but…"

"I'm going to go to the bathroom. You go set up the pillows." I pat his arm again and take off down the hall behind a waddling Maria. As we walk, Maria asks how it's been going.

"Not bad. As you might have guessed, I have to pee a lot. And I've been getting cramps in my belly on and off all day."

Maria nods knowingly. "Like a squeezing?"

"Yeah. Like I did sit ups or something. Which, as you can imagine, is impossible in this condition." I wave toward my belly.

"Probably Braxton Hicks contractions," Maria says.

I nod. "Yeah. Dr. Babin mentioned them at my last visit."

"They're normal," Maria says. "But let him know if they become regular."

I nod. This is basically what Dr. Babin had told me.

A few minutes later (okay, a half hour later...twenty peeing pregnant women is no joke), we are all seated in a semi-circle around Maria and the other instructor—midwife Rosie Walker.

Rosie is wearing a beaded skirt, smells faintly of patchouli oil, and literally has a crown of flowers in her hair. I can tell it's taking all of Roger's strength not to whisper some comment to me. His face is twisted into a grimace that one might mistake for severe constipation if one didn't know Roger.

Rosie proceeds to tell us about how we're going to learn the stages of labor—she has glossy pictures to share with us that Maria will hold up—and how to breathe through those stages so that we don't need medication. I hear a grumble of protests around me. Most of the women have obviously decided *that* isn't going to happen, but I'm willing to give it a shot. After all, I can always get the drugs if I change my mind, right?

Rosie claps her hands together like she's a kindergarten teacher (who knows, maybe in a former life she *was* a kindergarten teacher) and announces that she is going to show us a video. She wheels over a cart with a TV on it from the corner and after poking at the VCR for several minutes— before a much more tech savvy Maria comes to rescue her— she starts the video.

The video that starts with a woman spread eagle on a table, screaming her bloody head off. My jaw drops and I feel hot and cold all at the same time, my heart racing, my palms sweating. My mouth dries up as abdomen tightens up and quickly relaxes, but I feel very off-kilter. The sounds from the video sound faint and far away, and I feel strangely...*spinny*.

Crap. I think I'm going to pass out again.

7

September

You are 7 months pregnant. Your baby is about the size of an eggplant. His or her eyelids are still closed, but the eyes underneath are moving around, dreaming and responding to sound. This is the beginning of your third trimester and you may be feeling like it is becoming a little more difficult to move around. Sleeping is also starting to get uncomfortable and your center of gravity is changing, making you more prone to tripping and falling. Be careful and be sure to wear slip resistant shoes (oh so sexy).

You also may start feeling tightening of your abdomen on and off. Chances are, these are practice contractions called Braxton Hicks. They are nothing to worry about, but check with your doctor if they start to become regular and painful. You will definitely feel the baby moving around at this point in time...mostly when you're trying to sleep. It's like a rock concert is going on in the middle of the night in there. It may feel as if he or she is moshing on your organs, especially your bladder. If you are finding that sleep is too difficult, try sleeping in a reclining chair...it may help!

****

"Mrs. Maxwell, you really must drink more water. It can cause contractions if you get dehydrated," Maria clucks at me as she hooks me up to a baby heart rate monitor. She was the one who ushered me into one of the hospital exam rooms after passing out in class.

"I have," I insist as I feel my abdomen tighten up. I really have been drinking a lot of water. These Braxton Hicks contractions are annoying. It makes me feel like I have to pee even more.

"You wouldn't have passed out in an air conditioned room if you were drinking enough water," Maria scoffs.

"She goes to the bathroom every twenty minutes," Roger interjects. "I don't know how she can't be drinking enough water."

As I watch Roger pace the room, chewing his fingernails, I know this has probably has nothing to with drinking water. It's all the shock I've absorbed today— seeing Troy stealing packages, buying a house, watching a poor tortured soul give birth. Okay, maybe the last one was completely on TV, but still, that was the shock that put me over the edge.

But I definitely can't tell Roger or Maria that. I can't tell anyone that. I am completely alone in this. For some reason this brings tears to my eyes. I've been an emotional wreck lately, crying over the stupidest things. A few of the women on Baby Days mentioned having the same problem. It must be a side effect of pregnancy. As if being the size of a house in the middle of the summer and carrying a small person who likes to move around when you were trying to sleep, needs any additional side effects.

I used to tell Roger everything. I remember when we first started dating and Roger and I would spend every night on the phone, talking into the wee hours of the morning. I told him everything, and he shared things with me that his guy friends would have probably mocked him for—you know, for actually being a sensitive sort of person.

But ever since I got pregnant, I have discovered that I am hiding things from him. It's almost like this baby has cleaved us into two people again, Roger and Amy, instead of RogerandAmy, like we were for the first couple years together. As much as I want to spill my guts to him, about everything that's bothering me, something is holding me back.

Probably because I know he would absolutely insist that I leave the issue with Troy alone. And he might even tell me to quit my job. Not that he would force me to do it or anything archaic and caveman-ish like that, but he would be worried about me. And I don't want him to be worried about me. He's got enough on his mind worrying about the finances, and the fact that he's going to be working for an idiot Boy Boss come September. Plus, when he worries about me, he does rash things...like call my mother to tell her I've passed out.

Oh yeah, true story. When I passed out, he called my mother and told her to get to the hospital right away because it was an emergency and I might be in labor.

"I didn't know what to do, Amy!" he had cried after he confessed and I snapped at him. My mother was the *last* person I wanted around me when I was uncomfortable. And, I wasn't going into labor, so I really didn't need her there panicking about it, either. This was something she never even needed to know about—instead, she has a front row seat for the circus. Not to mention, she'll probably set a timer every day to call me at intervals and remind me to drink more freaking water. Ughhhhhhh.

"Mrs. Maxwell. Mr. Maxwell." Dr. Babin sweeps into the room, peering at my chart in his gnarled grandfatherly-like hands. He looks up and notices my mother sitting in the corner clutching her purse in her lap. My mother is done up in her usual "middle-class-aging-housewife-just-left-the-beauty-salon" style and she catches Dr. Babin's eye, causing him to break out in a broad grin. "*Well* who do we have here?" He leans toward my mother, almost bowing.

Maria snorts with disgust, but Dr. Babin doesn't seem to notice. To his credit, in his present line of work, he probably doesn't interact with many women in his own age demographic. Although my mother *is* only in her fifties, so he's still probably old enough to be her father. I shiver at the thought. Roger thinks I'm cold and starts manically tucking stray sheets around my body. I'm hot and feel like my skin is on fire, but I don't have the heart to shake the sheets off. I've already upset him enough today as it is.

"I'm Amy's mother," Mom says in a voice that can only be described as smoker with a head cold trying to sound sexy.

"Well, hello Mommy Maxwell," Dr. Babin gushes as he takes her hand in his. My mother's last name is *not* Maxwell.

My mother doesn't correct him. Instead, she giggles like a school girl as Dr. Babin presses her hand to his lips like some old-timey movie. Maria now snorts even louder and I can see her roll her big green eyes. She catches my eye and makes a gagging motion, causing me to laugh.

My laughter apparently causes Dr. Babin to remember that I, the patient, am in the room. "Ahh, yes. The lovely Mrs. Maxwell." He spins on his heel and takes my hand in his and kisses it as well, acting as if this is what he does at every appointment, and his attention to my mother isn't some anomaly. Roger glowers at him, but says nothing.

"What seems to be the problem today?" Dr. Babin asks with a concerned frown.

"She passed out at the birthing class," Roger tells him.

"Again," Maria adds in her thick brogue, causing my mother to bolt upright in her chair. I scowl at Maria. *Doesn't she have a birthing class to go to?*

"*Again*?" my mother squeaks. "What does she mean by *again,* Amy?" I don't reply. Instead I act as if I am fascinated by the ceiling tiles.

"Amy passed out at work about a month ago," Roger says through gritted teeth. I smack him in the arm and he shoots me a pleading expression. I guess given the option of choosing between pissing my mother off and pissing me off, pissing me off was the lesser of two evils.

"Why didn't someone tell me about the *first* time she passed out?" Mom squeezes that purse like a lemon she's trying to juice. She directs this toward me, her ire falling on my shoulders...as usual.

I pinch the fleshy part of Roger's bicep and he winces, but doesn't cry out. He knows he deserves it. He should have just kept his mouth shut to begin with. There was no reason to call my mother in the first place.

"This sort of thing happens all the time. Especially in the summer months," Dr. Babin interrupts, temporarily saving me from my mother's wrath. Still, there is no doubt in my mind that she will bring this up again later—how *much* later, no one knows. Mom hates being left out of the loop. Especially when she has been deprived of a chance to admonish me about something in the process. She will mentally file this transgression to later be used against me…quite possibly on her death bed.

"Dehydration," Maria says knowingly.

"Yes," Dr. Babin agrees as he eyes the monitor. "There are some contractions, though. So let's also do an internal and make sure nothing is going on. I want to make sure those contractions aren't doing something."

"Doing something?" I'm not sure what *something* is. Is something bad?

"Not to worry, dear." He pats my leg as he lowers himself onto the stool at the base of the exam table. "Scoot down here so I can do an internal."

I glance nervously at all the people in the room. Normally an internal exam wouldn't make me this leery, but I have yet to have one with such a large audience. I doubt Roger being in the room is what's making me nervous, though. I'm pretty sure it's my mother's rapt staring that makes me want to fold myself up and disappear.

"Um, maybe, Mom you should…" I trail off. I glance toward the door, hoping she will follow my eyes and take a hint, excusing herself in the process.

"I should do *what*, Amy?" Mom sniffs indignantly.

I must have hesitated a beat too long because Maria laughs, understanding my apprehension. "Ah, love. You better get used to it. This is a teaching hospital. Giving birth here is like being on stage."

Roger clears his throat uncomfortably. "I can go into the waiting room if you want." He rises to his feet and starts to walk away, but I grab his arm, accidentally digging my nails into his skin. The prenatal vitamins have worked wonders on them, so they're pretty long and lethal.

"Ouch!" he moans, grabbing at his own arm. "What'd you do that for?"

"I'm sorry. Please stay here," I apologize through tears that are now pricking my eyes. The wheels are falling off this bus at a rapid pace and I feel like I'm the bus driver losing control.

I pull at Roger's arm, bringing his ear to my mouth. "Get her *out,*" I hiss, my mood switching like a light. I'm back to angry.

Roger is momentarily confused. "The baby or your mother?"

"Huh?" I have no idea what he's talking about.

"You said *her.* I didn't know if you were talking about the baby or your mother," Roger explains…a little too loudly.

"The baby is a girl? Why didn't you tell me?" My mother gasps and clutches her chest like she's having a heart attack. Who knows…maybe the shock of discovering her daughter has kept secrets from her is enough to cause an older person to actually have a heart attack. Instantly, I am flooded with feelings of guilt.

"Yes, sorry Mom. We wanted it to be a surprise." I shoot Roger a look, daring him to tell my mother otherwise. Everyone else knew the baby was a girl…it had slipped my mind to tell my mother, though. Oops. I blame it on pregnancy brain.

"Okay, well can you please slide down here, Mrs. Maxwell," Dr. Babin says, sounding impatient for the first time since I met him.

"Um, yeah. Of course." I decide to ignore the emotional discomfort of having my mother in the room for this extremely personal experience, and just concentrate on the *actual* discomfort of this personal experience. Dr. Babin slips on his rubber gloves, snapping the ends as he does, causing me to shudder.

Dr. Babin gently inserts his fingers and I try not to gasp. I try not to pay any attention to the fact that an elderly man with a miner's helmet and a pair of rubber gloves is digging around inside my cooch in front of my mother and husband.

"So, how about those Mets?" I say with a chuckle. "They're looking good this year. They may actually have a shot at going to the World Series."Roger looks befuddled. "The season is almost over, Amy. There's no way they can get the Wild Card now. It's mathematically impossible."

My mother tuts—I'm not sure if she's commenting on our conversation, or she's in disbelief that we are actually having this conversation while I'm being prodded like a farm animal.

"Oh my," Dr. Babin says, face contorting into a grimace.

"Oh my?" I sit up slightly, forgetting that the doctor's fingers are attached to me. That causes a sharp pain, but the look on the doctor's face alarms me too much to actually care about the pain.

"Looks like you've started dilating, my dear. And you're fifty percent effaced as well." He clucks his tongue.

"What does that mean?" I ask, panic rising in my chest.

"It means," Dr. Babin says as he pulls off his gloves and tosses them into the small wastebasket in the corner of the room, "that we're going to have to admit you to the hospital so we can stop this labor."

"What?" Roger, me, *and* my mother say at the same time.

Dr. Babin nods solemnly. "Yes. You're only thirty weeks. We've got to keep this baby cooking for a little longer. I'm going to send you to the other side of the L&D floor. I'm off call in about a half hour, but my colleague Dr. Herman will take care of you over there."

Dr. Babin leaves the room after giving Maria instructions to let L & D know we are on our way. I sit up when they leave and look at both my husband and mother, both with equally dazed expressions on their faces.

****

I getting settled into a bed in a spacious room with several beds and monitors. Thankfully I am the only patient in the room right now because my mother is speaking rather loudly.

"All I'm saying is that you could have been more careful with the wheelchair. You almost ran over two nurses." My mother is wiggling her finger at Roger.

I see Roger grit his teeth. Mom and Roger haven't always gotten along so well, mostly due to my mother's insistence that *I could do better,* and because she didn't understand why we needed to *rush into getting married when you're so young.* Me being the young person, not Roger. He's fourteen years older than I am, another reason my mother wasn't a fan. She assumed he always had nefarious intentions with me. Like an aging vampire count or something.

Roger has generally been a polite and dutiful son-in-law, with the one exception being the night he got rip-roaring drunk at my sister's engagement party and basically called my mother a snob. Not to her face, of course, but she heard him nevertheless. She had been slinking around the side of the pool, eavesdropping on Roger's conversation with Beth's fiancé Derek. During this conversation Roger warned him to stay in my mother's good graces because she was a snob. Needless to say, she did not take it well.

Mom is now settling down in a chair next to my bed. She has taken a pad out of her giant purse, and has announced she is making a list of things for Roger to do if I need to stay at the hospital tonight. Phone calls for him to make, clothes for him to retrieve, etc. etc.

From the way Roger's jaw is clenched, I can tell he's trying not to go postal on her. I seriously wish I could tell her to go home. But my father has been unreachable since he dropped her off—he's probably celebrating freedom after being trapped in the house with her for two months, waiting for his suspension to be over—so there would be no way for her to get home. Her only choice would be to call a yellow cab, and she absolutely swears she would never lower her standards enough to get into one of them.

I actually chuckle to myself at the thought of her sitting on a bench outside the hospital with her purse on her lap, indignantly waiting for a yellow cab with sticky seats to come retrieve her and her linen pantsuit.

"Whatever is so funny, Amy?" my mother sniffs as she digs through her purse for a pen. "I'm going to write all this down for you Roger. So you don't forget."

I reach over the side of the bed and place my hand on Roger's knee which is now bouncing up and down. He glances at me and I give him a reassuring smile while widening my eyes and rolling them, acknowledging the fact that my mother is a nut job. I also mouth the words *loco en la cabeza,* knowing that even if my mother could read lips, she would have no idea what I was saying. Roger studied five years of Spanish between high school and college and can speak it pretty well. I took two years of French, but all I can remember is *tu vas au lit avec moi*? One of my boyfriends in high school used to whisper it in my ear. It sounded so sexy coming from his mouth that it used to give me goosebumps. I didn't even question what he said until I took French my junior year. It means, loosely translated, *will you go to bed with me?*

Roger offers me a grateful smile and stops bouncing, but he doesn't reply to my mother. I have a feeling that he would have some pretty choice words for her if he could actually speak right now.

By the time the nurse brings me a hospital gown and I have changed into it, I have some choice words for her myself. She has all but insinuated that I have completely brought this trip to the hospital upon myself by my, and I quote, "utter disregard for the maternal condition", whatever the heck that means.

As we wait for the nurse to take my information, my mother is currently droning on about how she kept her feet up for nine months and didn't engage in anything more strenuous than a sponge bath when she was pregnant with me and my sisters.

I roll my eyes and resist the urge to mention that she also drank gin and tonics when she was pregnant because "this was the seventies" and "they didn't know any better" and it "helped her relax". I discovered these fun facts from Aunt Sylvia, my mother's best friend, several Christmases ago when she was drunk. My mother was mortified and likes to pretend that Sylvia made the whole thing up. It hasn't stopped me from using it against her any time she mentions a "stupid decision" on my part. I always remind her that if I make stupid decisions, it's probably because she drank when she was pregnant. She gets flustered and usually shuts up.

I don't think *anything* will shut her up today. I pray that the nurse will tell her she has to leave when she hooks me up to the device to monitor my contractions and start the IV medication that promises to halt them, but alas, they let her stay.

After I am on the monitor for about a half an hour and ready to strangle my mom with the IV tubing, (Roger has managed to escape to the car because he forgot to put the ticket on the dashboard—a likely excuse), a tall blonde woman pulls back the curtain that's separating me from the rest of the open room.

"Hellooooo!" she calls out as if I am all the way across the room and not four feet away from her. "Mrs. Maxwell! It is soooo lovely to finally meet you!" She grasps my hand and enthusiastically pumps it, causing the monitor attached to my abdomen to beep rapidly.

"Ooops! My bad," she says in a sing-song voice. She readjusts the straps and puts her finger to her lips. "Shhhh. Don't tell the nurses."

"Um, hi," I reply. I'm not sure who this woman is, but it seems like I should know who she is from the way she's greeting me.

"And who are you exactly?" my mother asks in a haughty voice. Of course. Leave it to my mother to ask the difficult questions.

"Why, I'm Dr. Herman! Amy's obstetrician!"

Oh. This is the elusive Dr. Herman. Finally. She is not at all what I was expecting.

"Oh," my mother sniffs and begins to readjust the sheet over my abdomen. I really do not want the sheet covering me at all because I'm freaking hot as hell right now, but I'm not in the mood for a lecture on how I'll catch a chill and my baby will be born with a birthmark or something utterly ridiculous if I try to remove it.

"So, Mrs. Maxwell." Dr. Herman clasps her hands together as she speaks. "The plan is to monitor you while the Brethine is administered—"

"The what now?" My mother cocks her head to the side and peers disapprovingly at the doctor. She gets flustered when she can't understand what people are talking about since she considers herself to be an educated woman.

"Brethine. It's a drug used to halt premature labor." Dr. Herman taps the plastic bag hanging from the IV pole. "Now it does have some potentially unpleasant side effects—"

"Is it really necessary then?" Mom interrupts.

Dr. Herman wrinkles her brow as if she doesn't understand my mother. "Is what really necessary?"

"This Brethine," my mother says, sweeping her hands toward the IV bag of medication. "Can't labor be stopped some other way? Like tilting her on her head or something? It can't be good for the baby to have drugs in her system."

Says the educated woman who drank gin and tonics while pregnant. Three times.

Dr. Herman smiles warmly and grabs my mother's hands, eliciting a yelp from Mom. She does not like to be touched by strangers. Heck, she doesn't even like to be touched by her own children.

"I assure you that this is the best possible solution to the problem, erm...Mrs…"

"Mrs. Porter. I'm Amy's mother," Mom huffs, withdrawing her hands. I really hope she doesn't go into a tirade about "her day". I won't be able to resist bringing up the gin and tonics.

"Pleasure to meet you," Dr. Herman says politely, although I am certain it is anything but. "Anyway," she continues, turning her attention back to me. "After this is complete, we will monitor you for twenty-four hours and make sure everything is okay."

"Twenty-four hours?" I squeak. "Like overnight?" In all my life, I have never spent a night in the hospital, and the idea of doing it now terrifies me. Obviously I have not given any thought to the idea that I would be spending the night, or rather, several nights in the hospital when the baby was born. That was going to be a "cross that bridge when we come to it" situation.

"Twenty-four hours?" Roger's panicked voice echoes my sentiments from the doorway.

"I *told* you this was a possibility," Mom says as she waves the pad in the air triumphantly. *Hence the lists.*

"Like I said, side effects may occur and it's best to be in a hospital where it can be fixed quickly."

Roger looks ill. "We're waiting for a call from the realtor—"

"Relax, Roger," Mom says with a shake of her head. Her hair doesn't even move. I have no idea how she manages that—it's like it's spackled to her head. "*You* won't be stuck here for twenty-four hours. *You* get to go home. Poor Amy will be the one stuck in a hospital bed for twenty-four hours."

She tuts and pats my hand as if this makes me pathetic. It makes me feel even more upset about this whole situation. Tears start to well in my eyes, and I bite my lip hard to prevent myself from crying in front of my mother.

"Yes. *Everyone* needs to go home," Dr. Herman says, probably sensing the tension in the room. "Mrs. Maxwell needs her rest. You can all come back in the morning when she's ready to be discharged. There's really nothing to be gained by hanging around here. In fact, the cafeteria isn't even open anymore," she remarks, glancing at the watch on her wrist.

My mother rises to her feet and pulls her purse over her shoulder with a sigh worthy of a martyr. "I guess that's true, isn't it, Roger? I'll be needing a ride home. I can't reach your father-in-law. I'll give you a copy of the list—I've also made a copy for myself in case you lose it."

Roger nods dutifully, but I can tell he is severely distressed by the notion that he has to drive in the car with my mother for twenty minutes without me as a buffer. I send him an apologetic look as he leans down to kiss me.

"Please forgive me if I push her out of the moving vehicle," he whispers.

I laugh. "We never had this conversation. I know nothing."

He pulls away with a smile, just as Dr. Herman remarks, "Oh, and just so you know, once you go home, you're going to have to be on bedrest until you reach thirty-six weeks." She consults my chart. "So about six weeks of bedrest."

My jaw (along with Roger's) drops open.

Crap. How am I supposed to catch Troy the package thief if I'm on bedrest?

7.5

Maxwell Mommy: *I got some bad news at the doctor this week.*

Bun in the Oven: *Oh no! What happened?*

Maxwell Mommy: *Well, I got put on bedrest. Apparently the contractions that I thought were Braxton Hicks contractions were real.*

George's Gal: *Wow! That's scary!*

Maxwell Mommy: *It really was. They started off blaming it on dehydration, but then the doctor realized that it was more than that.*

Mum 2B: *I can't imagine being dehydrated. I must drink 20 liters of water a day. Which makes me have to wee every twenty minutes.*

She's Having My Baby: *Oh my wife does too. So annoying when we're driving somewhere.*

In a Baby Daze: *So sorry she inconveniences you, pal. You know what's really annoying? Inconsiderate jerks that knocked you up and don't stop when you have to go to the bathroom.*

Mum 2B: *Well good luck on the bedrest thing. There's no way I could do bedrest with a 3 year old at home.*

Eating 4 2: *I'm supposed to be on bedrest, too! But I have a two year old so there is no way I can even stay still for ten minutes. I try to get her to take a nap so I can at least sit down, but she won't have it!*

Mom to 3: *Bedrest is no joke! You need to take the health of your baby seriously!*

****

A few weeks after I end up on bedrest, we are scheduled to close on the house in Dayville. The whole thing happened rather quickly.

We had gotten the call that our offer was accepted while I was in the hospital. Eva left a message on the machine. But Roger didn't realize we had a message on the machine because he didn't know what the blinking light was for. He actually thought it was to let us know the phone was working.

Therefore, we didn't get the message until I got home and noticed the light blinking. Roger sheepishly listened to the message when I explained how to retrieve it. That resulted in a whirlwind of activity—Roger scurrying around the house with paperwork for me to sign, my dad dropping off enough cardboard boxes to pack up Buckingham Palace, my mother packing stuff up and refusing to let me lift anything, and the puppy running around under foot and getting stepped on at least three times a day.

Roger has been organizing the moving van and all the details for closing, including a home inspection. He went to the house last week and took pictures so I can tell him what color I want each room painted. I have not been to the house since I saw it on the day I ended up on bedrest. The day I saw Troy's truck and watched him take the neighbor's package.

Instead of helping, I lie on the couch with my feet up (at my mother's insistence...I'm sure she may spank me like she did when I was a child if I dare to set my feet on the floor). Not only am I unable to pack up my own belongings or help make my new house a home, I am plagued by the fact that I know Troy has been stealing packages, but I can't do anything about it, being immobile and all that.

I want to call Carol and ask her what she thinks, but I can't find the piece of paper that she wrote her cell phone number on. My mother probably threw it out in her flurry of packing activity. It's possible that Carol and Harry are still packing up the pharmacy, but I know my mother isn't going to let me take a walk or a ride down there. I couldn't possibly come up with a legitimate reason why I want to visit an empty pharmacy. And my mother will definitely bristle if I tell her I want to go hang out with Carol. She will give me a lecture about how I need to find friends my own age.

I can't tell my mother about the package theft, either. She most certainly won't approve of me trying to piece together this puzzle. As much as my mother loves to read mystery novels, she wants nothing to do with actual mysteries in real life. She has no tolerance for vigilante justice (as I discovered in third grade when I took matters into my own hands after a classmate started stealing from other classmate's sticker book—I brought that girl down. Literally. With a karate chop. Mom was mortified when she got called into the principal's office.)

Besides, she'll tell Roger what I'm up to and he *definitely* will want me to mind my own business. I doubt highly that he would want me investigating a felon on my own. I mean, I think it's a felony, right? At any rate, it's illegal activity, and I know that my husband would not want me tangled up in anything illegal.

I can just see him preaching now—*not only is it dangerous, Amy, but I'm a pillar of the community and I can't be associated with illegal activity...I could lose my job!* Then they would both tell me to call the police. And I can't call the police. They'll think I'm either A., nuts, or B., a stalker.

Plus the Package Stealing Bandit (as he has come to be known in the papers—how creative...not) is pretty low on the police's list of important cases lately. In addition to a package bandit, there are houses being burgled in the area left and right. It seems to happen every summer, though...when people go on vacation and leave their houses empty for long periods of time. The newspaper has been including tips on how to safeguard your house when you go on vacation almost every day lately.

Wait! The newspaper! Of course! That's it! I'll call the newspaper and tell them what I know. They can investigate it! Where's the phone?

This idea hits me at the same time that my mother dumps a pile of photos on my lap. "Why don't you have these pictures in albums, Amy?"

"I have them in a box, Mom. Where did the box go?"

My mother waves a broken shoebox in my face. "This box, Amy? This isn't meant to hold pictures. You have perfectly good photo albums in here!" She points to the stack of unopened photo albums on the desk.

I stare longingly at the desk and the cordless phone, just out of reach. My photo storage woes are the least of my worries today. I couldn't care less about photos right now.

I must say that out loud because my mother makes a wounded face and begins to lecture me about how I will care when my daughter is grown up and leaves home and doesn't ever call or visit and all I have is pictures to look at and cry. I have a feeling she's making this personal, but I'm too wrapped up in the Package Bandit mystery to even care. And I'm plotting how I will get ahold of the cordless phone to call the paper.

As Mom busies herself with putting photos in the albums, I glance up at the clock on the wall. It's almost five o'clock. I'm not sure what time the paper closes, or even who I can call to share the story with, but I don't think they're open all night. I also don't think my mother is going to let me move off the couch to go talk to a reporter out of earshot. She nearly lost her mind when I bent down to scratch my shin.

Then I see the pad and pen on the desk, and an idea starts to take shape in my head. *I can write a letter to the newspaper and mail it!*

"Hey, Mom?" I call out to her—she's dabbing her eyes, still looking at the pictures. What a productive use of time...*not.*

"Hey is for horses, young lady," she admonishes me, without even looking up from the photos. I roll my eyes.

"Excuse me. Hello, Mother?"

She scowls at me. "Yes?"

"Can you get me that pad and pen over there, please?" I ask sweetly, batting my eyelashes.

"This one?" My mother holds it up for me and I nod. "Are you making a list for Roger?"

Why does she automatically assume I'm always going to make a honey do list for my husband just because that's her go to form of torture for my dad? I want to snap out an enthusiastic no, but I also don't want her to ask me what I'm actually writing.

My mother claps her hands in delight after she hands me the pad and pen. "I just love lists, don't you? It makes everything so much easier when you're organized!"

I cringe. I *do* like making lists. But I will *not* tell my mother that and give her the satisfaction of thinking she passed down some desirable organization gene to me. I am still holding out hope that I'm adopted. Or that I was my father's mistress's kid, and my mother took pity on me and adopted me to raise as her own and that's why she likes my sisters more than she likes me.

Of course, *that's* unlikely because I've never known my mother to have an altruistic bone in her body, and taking on someone else's kid—your husband's mistress's kid, nonetheless—seems like something that you would have to be an altruistic sort to do. What am I even thinking? There is no mistress! My dad can't even tie his shoes without my mother knowing. She's such a nosy busybody...nothing escapes her attention.

I smile weakly and curl the pad toward my chest so that she can't see what I'm writing. Still, she plops down next to me and peppers me with questions.

"Is it a list of things to pack? Or is it a list of things he needs to do before the closing? You know you have to make sure that they get the C of O before the closing, right? Did he send all those notarized documents to the lawyer yesterday when he was supposed to? It'll set things back if they don't get it on time. You know, he really should have hand delivered those things." She makes a tsking noise. "Do you have copies? Roger should have made copies just in case something got lost in the mail. Or did he send it certified mail? You should always send important documents certified, that way no one can ever say you didn't send it. People can be absolutely sneaky about things and lie and say they didn't get something when they did. And of course, things can actually *get* lost in the mail. Did I ever tell you about the time your sister's college tuition check got lost in the mail? What a nightmare that was to sort out! They were going to kick her out! Can you imagine that? Your sister Beth, the smartest person I know, getting kicked out of college!"

I clench my fists. *Does she have to mention how smart Beth is every chance she can get? Or how Beth is so successful?*

I had enough of that while growing up. I don't need that now that I'm all grown up and independent and moved out of the house.

Besides, I got married before Beth did. And what's more, I'm having a baby before Beth is. Ha! Take that Beth!

As I glance around at the boxes my mother is packing up and recall how I'm virtually a prisoner in my own house, I realize that maybe I'm not as independent as I would actually like to be at the moment. I'm kind of beholden to my mother right now.

Fortunately, my mother is easily distracted by shiny objects (aka. more pictures) and I can begin my letter to the newspaper. I tap the pen against my lips, not sure what I should write. How does one begin the letter that may lead to a journalist's career skyrocketing into stardom? And who do I address it to?

I glance at the paper sitting on the floor (Mom was wrapping up picture frames earlier) and see Julia Heart's column staring back up at me. I went to school with her and her twin sister Jessica. While Jessica had been a popular cheerleader with a ton of friends and great hair, Julia had been the sad mousy haired nobody at the back of the room that everyone ignored. I had always felt bad for her—I knew exactly what it was like living in your sister's shadow. Even though I talked to Julia every once in a while in school, I stayed away for the most part and we were never friends.

Dear Julia,

I start the letter off and then immediately scratch out the greeting. No, dear Julia is a little too familiar. She probably doesn't even remember me from school, and I don't want to scare her off by sounding like I know her personally. I can't send this letter with words scratched off—Julia will never take me seriously.

I tear off the sheet of paper and crumble it into a ball, already annoyed with myself.

Dear Ms. Heart,

My name is Amy Maxwell. Perhaps you remember me as Amy Porter. I went to high school with you and your sister Jessica.

No. Wait. Why did I bring up Jessica? Maybe Jessica is a sore subject with her, and the second she reads her sister's name, she's going to toss the letter in the garbage without reading another word. And then I will have completely wasted my time and will not have accomplished anything.

I ball up the second attempt at the letter and start another version. I am two sentences in before I realize that maybe Julia *does* remember me and maybe she doesn't have fond memories of me. I don't want her to disregard my letter simply because she doesn't like me.

The third letter gets ripped up. I am now seriously annoyed at myself for not thinking this through before I started to write. I really wish I could get up and type the letter on the computer so that I wouldn't have to keep starting over, but then my mother would definitely be hovering over my shoulder reading my every word. Think, Amy! Think!

Ms. Heart,

I am writing as a concerned citizen of Morningside. I have lived here all of my life and I have pride in this town. I often frequent our small businesses as I think they are the backbone of this town.

As you know by now, there has been a rash of theft among the small businesses and homeowners in this community and in Dayville as well. The police have made substandard attempts to investigate, and have not resolved the issue that has been plaguing this town and neighboring town for the last few months. I believe that they are not really interested in solving these crimes because with minimal investigation as an ordinary citizen, I have been able to hone in on a viable suspect.

His name is Troy Lewis and he works at the Morningside Animal Shelter as an animal control officer. I saw the back of his van filled with suspicious packages once when I went out to his truck to give him something he had forgotten inside. I also spotted him removing a package from an elderly woman's porch in Dayville. Dayville has their own Animal Shelter so there was no reason for him to be there. He also does not know the elderly woman whose package he took. He stole it, plain and simple.

I am hesitant to go to the police about what I know since I don't think they are taking this crime spree as seriously as they should be. I was hoping that you could use your journalistic investigation skills and look into this matter yourself. Imagine solving this mystery...you would be a hero in the eyes of everyone in this community.

Sincerely,

A Concerned Citizen

I reread the letter to myself and nod my head, satisfied that I have hit all my important talking points and that Julia will have no choice but to investigate. After all, it's what a good journalist would do, right?

As I ponder that, I realize that I don't even know if Julia *is* a good journalist. In fact, chances are, she's mediocre at best. After all, she's working for the rinky-dinky hometown newspaper in the community where she grew up in. And from what I can see, she's mostly writing fluff articles on which plants do best in direct sunlight and how to get grass stains out of white pants. She's actually a step down from the Dear Heloise column. At least that lady is nationally syndicated.

Still, I don't know if anyone else at the paper would even acknowledge my letter. Contacting Julia is the best shot at getting someone to look into this crime.

Satisfied, I fold up the paper and gaze longingly at the desk. The envelopes and stamps are in the top drawer on the right, but my mother is blocking any chance I have of getting my hands on them. I am going to have to wait until she goes to the bathroom or something. Which probably wouldn't be for a while, considering she is like a camel when it comes to that sort of thing. She had always been annoyed with Beth, Joey, and me whenever we would have to go to the bathroom upon entering a store or starting a road trip. She never seemed to have to go. She yelled at us for drinking too much all the time. Which is ironic considering that I was yelled at a bazillion times the last few weeks because I wasn't drinking enough.

As I suspected, Mom spends the next hour organizing the photos. It would have taken her much less time if she hadn't looked at every single photo and waved it in my face with a commentary or a question.

But finally, just before six o'clock, I get my chance. Mom stands up and stretches, heading over to the front closet to pack up what is left in there. The puppy bounds to her feet, non-existent tail wagging, tongue lolling happily from her mouth. Poor thing. She probably thinks my mother is taking her for a walk since we keep her leash in the front closet. The puppy hasn't been for a decent walk since I've been on bedrest. Roger takes her out on the common area lawn first thing in the morning (carefully avoiding any other resident in case they report us to the association) and last thing at night so that she can do her business, but he's too busy and too tired to take her any farther than that.

That's when I realize that I don't have to wait for my mother to go to the bathroom—forget waiting for the camel to have to relieve herself. I can ask her to take the puppy outside for a walk. That'll be more than enough time to grab the envelope off the desk, address it, and stick a stamp on it.

"Mom?" I ask as she reenters the room, dog on her heels, yelping away with delight. My mother has a stack of newspapers in her hand, Julia Heart's somber picture staring up at me from the bottom of the stack. Underneath her picture is the address where I can send correspondence. My mother has unknowingly helped me kill two birds with one stone. I now have Julia's address, as well as a means to get up and walk across the room for an envelope without getting yelled at.

"Yes?" My mother flicks a stray hair off of her forehead. The air in the apartment is humid, despite the fact that the air conditioner is roaring full blast. My mother's usually well-coiffed hair is damp with sweat and sticking to her head.

"Can you take Misty for a short walk? I think she has to go to the bathroom." I indicate to the dog who is dancing on her hind legs. She just wants to go for a walk, but my mother might think the dance is one of pee pee urgency, and I know she doesn't want to end up cleaning up a puddle of puppy pee.

"Ugh, I guess," she grumbles, setting the newspapers down.

"Her leash is in the closet," I say with a thankful smile. "She's used to me walking her a few times a day. Poor thing is probably going crazy cooped up all day." I don't mention that the dog is not the only one going crazy being cooped up all day.

"This was a heck of a time to get a puppy, Amy." She clicks her tongue to make her disapproval of my choice to adopt the dog while pregnant and moving known. As if she hadn't voiced that disapproval with actual *words* on several occasions. Like I knew I was going to end up on bedrest or that we would be moving.

"Well, she'll have a fenced in yard soon enough when we move," I point out. The dog cocks her head to the side, left ear flopping. She begins to pant excitedly, like she's looking forward to having a fenced in yard to frolic in.

My mother doesn't say anything as she hooks up the jubilant puppy to her leash.

"Thanks."

"Ouch," Mom moans, rubbing her back. "All that packing isn't good for my back. I just can't pack like I used to." She shoots me a withering look.

"Sorry," I mutter, as if I have any control over her aging body and its inability to pack like she used to. I guess it's my fault that she's packing to begin with, but hello...I had no choice in the matter either. It's not like I'm lounging around eating bon-bons and watching Spanish soap operas with subtitles or something. (Okay, maybe I did that *one* day…)

But seriously, I would much rather be on my own two feet, packing up my house, and investigating my slimy co-worker to expose him for the creepy package thief that he is.

"Don't get off that couch," my mother warns with a waving finger before disappearing through the front doorway.

"I won't!" I lie as the door closes with a thud and I am met by the blessedly gorgeous sound of silence, my long lost friend that I had taken for granted for so many years.

I don't know how long my mother will walk the puppy for, but it should be long enough for me to retrieve the envelope off the desk and address it.

Using the couch as leverage, I catapult myself to my feet, nearly falling on my face in the process. I shakily grab the arm of the couch, forgetting that I haven't been moving lately and I am really unsteady on my feet. Not to mention the fact that I'm lugging a bowling ball around in my belly on top of it.

Getting my bearings, I lumber unsteadily over to the desk and pull open the drawer. As predicted, there is a stack of envelopes right inside the drawer. I take one and stuff the letter I wrote into it. Grabbing the newspaper, I locate Julia's address. As I am addressing the envelope, my hands are shaking. I feel like a foreign spy on an espionage mission in a European country during World War Two, instead of a pregnant woman addressing a letter to a newspaper columnist in her own living room. Still, a mission is a mission. And the danger associated with Mom discovering me on this mission could be just as harrowing.

My next mission is to find a stamp. They are not with the envelopes as I originally suspected. Digging through the drawers in the desk, I realize that this may be the more difficult part of this task. I have no idea where Roger keeps the stamps, or if we even *have* stamps at all in the house.

My heart is hammering in my chest when I hear the thud of the door downstairs. My mother is returning already and I haven't completed my mission! I have barely enough time to get back to the couch before she arrives, and I still haven't found the stamps!

Panicking, I go to shove the addressed envelope into drawer where Roger keeps the checkbook, and a scalloped edge sticking out of the checkbook catches my eye. *A stamp!*

Glancing at the door as if I'm expecting my mother bypass the stairs and fly up here, I snatch the stamp from the checkbook. I lick it quickly, paste it on the envelope, and then slide the envelope into the drawer. I race back to my spot on the couch, clutching my belly as if the baby is going to fall out.

As I huff and puff—hey, this is more cardiovascular activity than I've done in weeks...they barely let me lift my own toothbrush—it has just dawned on me that I'm going to have to figure out how to *mail* this envelope. Our mail is delivered into little boxes in the vestibule of the apartment by the mailman, not to a mailbox on our front porch where I can simply deposit the envelope and expect the mailman to take it back to the post office. There is, however, a mailbox on the corner, about a half a block from our apartment building.

As my mother sweeps into the house like a tornado, legs getting tangled up in the enthusiastic puppy's leash, I realize that I need *another* plan to get her out of the apartment...something that will get her out for longer than a quick walk around the block. Something that will give me enough time to get to the mailbox on the corner without being caught.

Now, you might be wondering why I don't just do whatever I want to do, being a grown woman and all that. Well, you haven't met my mother. My mother, a diminutive woman of five foot two inches tall with hair that looks like it has been molded onto her head in the shape of a helmet, is actually one the most terrifying people that I have ever met.

She can reduce a grown man (my dad) to tears with her signature withering look. She certainly scared the crap out of me when I was a kid—and not just in a normal mom way. I was terrified to cross her.

In fact, when I was nine, I forgot to throw out my egg salad sandwich at school (like I did every single day) and found that it was still in my lunchbox when I got home. I knew Mom would smell it if I threw it out in the kitchen garbage, and quite possibly kill me for not eating it (along with giving me a lecture about starving children in Africa), so I flushed it down the toilet. I can assure you that *that* didn't work out quite as I had envisioned it either, my father taking apart the toilet and cursing under his breath at eleven o'clock at night.

When Dad realized what had happened, he just gave me his own look and told my mother that one of her damn tampons had clogged up the toilet. We were in this together, me and him. He wasn't going to throw me to the wolves. I never forgot his generosity.

That's it! That's how I'll mail the letter! Dad!

When my father comes to retrieve my mother after Roger gets home, I can ask him to mail the letter for me. He'll do it, no questions asked. Not like my mother who would most likely steam the envelope open to check its contents if I ask *her* to mail it. And then she would rat me out to Roger who would flip his lid about how I shouldn't be getting involved and blah, blah, blah, pillar of the community, blah, blah, blah.

"My God, Amy, this dog is a handful," Mom gasps as she pats her hair down with her brightly manicured hand. My mother unhooks the leash and hangs it back in the closet. As if to demonstrate how incredibly incorrect my mother's statement is, Misty plops down demurely on the carpet and rests her head against her fuzzy paws. She glances up at me with her melty chocolate puppy dog eyes as if to say, *who me?*

I know better than to argue with my mother, though. "Thanks for walking her."

She nods and returns to the desk chair, dangerously close to the letter that I don't want her to know about. "Why are you panting, Amy? You didn't get up and move about while I was out, did you?" She eyes me like a lawyer interrogating a criminal in a courtroom.

I swallow hard and pick at the Native American blanket that I have haphazardly thrown across my legs. "I'm just overheated, that's all. It's very hot today."

"Well, take that blanket off," she chastises with an eye roll. "My goodness, you can't figure *that* out?"

I guiltily toss the blanket to the side. Mom starts wrapping up the picture frames with the newspaper, so I casually ask, "So when is Dad coming to pick you up?"

Mom shakes her head. She's holding my wedding picture in a silver frame in one hand and a handful of newspaper in the other. "He's not. He had to take the car to the mechanic. Beth is picking me up on her way home from work."

I resist the urge to groan. There is no way that my holier-than-thou sister Beth would ever mail something for me without an interrogation that would be similar to my mother's. I swear she's my mother's clone.

My mother, not realizing she has completely ruined my plans, goes back to wrapping up frames and sticking them in boxes. I go back to plotting to mail the letter. Yes, I realize that my life has now moved on from the *boring as watching paint dry* category, to the *sadder than an eighty-year-old spinster with nine cats watching re-runs of game shows* category.

I don't come up with a plan before my mother is picked up by Beth, who of course comes up.

Beth: (air kisses my mother) Hi, Mom! You look wrecked, you poor dear!

Mom: (sighs) I am. I'm just about wrung out from all this packing.

Beth: Oh, I know what you mean! I've had such a crazy day! Non-stop court action! I didn't even stop for lunch! It's fortuitous that we had a power outage at work or I wouldn't have even left until midnight! (laughs in that annoying way of hers)

Mom: Oh that's terrible! You must be starving!

Me: Hi, Beth.

Beth: (eyes widening as she turns to face me) Oh hi, Amy! I didn't even see you all tucked away on the couch. You look like a lady of leisure with your feet up over there! (laughing)

Me: I assure you, I am not a lady of leisure.

Beth: (ignores me) Oh, how I would love to sit with my feet up with such insouciance!

She's really upping the ante on the "big words" today—how very passive aggressive of her.

Me: (dripping with sarcasm and sweat) I'm having a ball.

Beth: (perching on the edge of the couch) It must be so difficult for you watching Mommy do all this work while you can't even help at all. I'm sure it's so disconcerting to know that her exhaustion is due to *your* medical condition!

Me: (through gritted teeth while pinching my thighs so I don't punch her in the face) Yup.

Beth: (clasps her hands together) Well, Mommy…I suggest *you* do what *I'm* going to do when I get home. Have a nice glass of Chablis and relax in the hot tub.

Mom: I'm too tired even for that today—

Beth: (pats me on the arm) Oh, I shouldn't have mentioned that, Amy. You can't have a drink or go in the hot tub, right? Are you craving a drink? My friend Denise craved Coronas the whole time she was pregnant and she doesn't even drink beer!

I don't hear anything else she says because she has given my brain some food for thought, and a new plot is cooked up. A drink is exactly how I'm going to get to the mailbox.

No! Not an alcoholic beverage…although after being trapped in the house with my mother packing up all my belongings the past few days makes me long for a glass of wine.

"Hey, Roger?" I say slyly after my mother and Beth have gone. Roger is contemplating the pizza delivery menu. I don't even know why he's bothering to look. We've had the same pizza delivered for the past four days now, a half pepperoni and sausage, half pineapple and mushroom pie. The first half for Roger and the second for me. And yes, pineapple *does* belong on pizza. I'm surprised the pizza delivery guy hasn't already showed up with our pie—it's about a half hour later than we've been ordering it.

"Hmmmm," Roger muses as he flips over the menu, inspecting the back, as if it has suddenly changed in the last twenty-four hours.

"I don't think I want pizza tonight."

Roger lowers the menu and stares at me as if I have told him that I don't think I remember my own name. "What? What are we going to eat?"

"I could really go for a milkshake from Tommy's."

"Tommy's?" Roger wrinkles up his brow as if I'm speaking a foreign language now.

Tommy's is a diner/ice cream parlor five miles away. When we were kids, my parents used to take us to Tommy's any time we had some minor accomplishment—dance recital, good report card, spring concert, soccer games. Dad even took me and my sisters there a couple of times on a random weeknight just because. I have not had a milkshake from Tommy's in months. The last time we went to Tommy's was before Roger's interview for the principal position that he didn't get.

"You can't go to Tommy's," Roger says, aghast. "You're on bedrest!"

I laugh. "I know I'm on bedrest. But you're not. Can you go get me a milkshake? I've been craving one all day. And you can get those disco fries you love," I say with a saccharine smile. I know Roger's exhausted from working all day, but can he really deprive his pregnant wife of a milkshake?

"Fine. But it's going to take me some time. It's a ten minute drive there and a ten minute drive back. You'll be by yourself that whole time." He cocks his head and speaks as if

I am five years old and the idea of being by myself for that length of time is terrifying.

"I'm a big girl, Roger. I told you that last week. I don't need a babysitter twenty-four seven."

And if I didn't *have* a babysitter twenty-four seven, I might have been able to make headway on this Package Bandit problem. I would have at least been able to use the phone to call Julia Heart today at any rate.

Roger sighs. "I wasn't going to be the one to argue with your mother about babysitting you," he says as he grabs his keys. "Chocolate?" he asks, but he doesn't need to ask. He knows what I like.

I nod, and like that, he's out the door.

Once again, I'm met with silence and it's the greatest noise in the world. Knowing Roger will be gone awhile, I am not in panic mode like I was earlier when left alone. This time I can actually hear myself think for the first time in weeks. I rise to my feet unsteadily and stretch out my back, groaning in the process. Misty looks up with concern. She gets to her feet and cocks her head to the side as she tends to do.

"It's okay, girl," I tell her as I practically limp over to the desk and retrieve my letter from the drawer. I then head to hall closet where my mother deposited Misty's leash earlier. "It's your lucky day! We're going for *another* walk."

At the sound of her second favorite word on the planet (her first is *dinner*) the puppy bounds over to me and nearly knocks me on my butt with her exuberance.

"Calm down," I laugh, clipping the leash to her collar. "We're only going to the mailbox on the corner."

The puppy doesn't seem to care as she pulls me into the hallway, the door slamming behind us. She tugs me down the stairs and I almost have to jog to catch up with her. This causes me to pant and hold my belly up as I move. I never understood why pregnant women seemed to be holding their babies in like that, but I guess it's instinct or something. I seriously have no idea why I'm doing it either.

We exit the building and just like that, I'm out on the sidewalk, free for the first time since my doctor's appointment earlier in the week. Now that I am on bedrest, I have to see the doctor weekly. Normally that would have annoyed me, sitting in the waiting area for a half hour or more, and then sitting in the exam room half naked for another half hour or so, but it was my only way out of the house at this point so I relished my weekly visits to Dr. Babin.

Even though it is nearly eight o'clock at night, the sky is still bright with daylight. I can see the mailbox, not too far from the entrance of the building, the sun actually glowing on it, like a beacon in the night.

Once on the sidewalk, I hurry over to the mailbox, looking left and right as if Roger or my mother will jump out of the shrubbery and chastise me for disobeying doctor's orders. As much as this newfound freedom is intoxicating, I don't want to risk getting caught and lectured. I will do this as quickly as possible, much to Misty's dismay.

After dropping the letter in the mailbox and checking five or six times to assure myself that it has indeed fallen to the bottom, I turn on my heel and shuffle back to the apartment building. It is only when I get to the door of the building that an awful realization occurs to me.

Crap. I forgot my key.

8

October

You are 8 months pregnant. You may feel like you're carrying around a small watermelon right at this point. And it's no wonder because your baby is only slightly smaller than a watermelon at eight months. The baby is fully formed at this point in time, with not too much "cooking" left to do. Now the baby will be gaining about a half a pound to a pound a week and even if he or she is born in this time frame, he or she should be healthy.

Still, you'll want to keep that baby in for the entire nine months for his or her best chance at life. The baby's lungs are not quite fully developed at this stage and every additional day helps assure a healthy baby. If you go into premature labor at this stage, your doctor will mostly likely still attempt to stop the labor by giving you medication and putting you on bedrest for the next few weeks until you reach 36 weeks. Even though this is difficult to cope with, remember, this is all for your baby.

Swelling could really be a problem now. Your feet are swelling, along with your hands. You might feel like a giant puffer fish! It's very important to keep up with your doctor's appointments (they're probably weekly now) so that the doctor can check your blood pressure. Swelling could be a sign of preeclampsia.

It may feel like you've been pregnant forever at this stage, but don't worry…it won't be much longer now!

****

"Amy? Is that you?"

Roger rapidly blinks his eyes in the darkness as he approaches the front of the apartment building, a Styrofoam cup in one hand and a bag soaked through with grease in the other.

I have been standing out in front of the building, praying that a fellow apartment dweller will come home before Roger. Fairly certain that I have not locked the door to the *actual* apartment, I was hoping someone would let me in the vestibule and I'd be able to slip upstairs and onto the couch before Roger got home.

Of course, that was not to be. It is Friday night and all of our fellow apartment dwellers are out for the evening.

"Did something happen?" Roger asks as he rushes toward me, face pale. "Did your water break? Do you have to go to the hospital? Should I call an ambulance?"

I don't think I've ever seen my husband quite this panicked. He should make an interesting birth coach when I actually do go into labor.

Since he has not seemed to notice Misty on her leash, I point her out, thankful to have her as an alibi. "Misty needed to go out," I lie. "And then I got stuck out here because I forgot my key."

"Oh," Roger says thoughtfully. He's thinking—probably considering yelling at me for taking the dog out. But then the realization that if I didn't take Misty out and she went to the bathroom inside the house he would be the one cleaning it up, dawns on him. "Let's get you inside."

He hands me the milkshake and sticks his key in the lock, turning it and pulling the door open. He holds it, allowing me and the puppy to step through. "You should take the elevator," he says sweeping his hand toward the ancient, creaky machine in the corner.

I shake my head vehemently. I hate elevators and the sounds that this one makes does not instill any confidence in me that the elevator can safely deliver me to my destination three floors above. Plus, this elevator doesn't work nine days out of ten.

"I'll be fine. It's just a few flights of stairs. And I don't think it's working. It's never working."

"You weren't supposed to even be out of the apartment," Roger grumbles. But I can tell he has been worn down today by work and whole house buying process. I was certainly wise to break free on *his* watch instead of my mother's. He just doesn't have the energy to fight me on this. My mother would have never let me forget it, droning on endlessly about how I risked *her* grandchild's life.

When we get back into the apartment, I ignore the twinges in my belly and the pain that is shooting up and down my back. There is no way in hell that I'm going to mention any of it to Roger. If I do, I'm sure he would draw a direct correlation between my pain and the fact that I ignored my orders of bedrest just now. And I'm trying to get *off* bedrest, not have more of it. In fact, next Saturday, I go back to the doctor and I will be 35 weeks pregnant. Dr. Babin told me I would be released from the confines of bedrest at 36 weeks since the baby will be full term at that point, but I'm planning to beg to come off a week early on account of good behavior—specifically, no further dilation.

I just have to figure out how to survive the next week on bedrest.

****

We close on the new house on Monday, and by Friday, everything has been packed into boxes. My mother has packed up the apartment within an inch of its life. I don't have a magazine to read or a TV to watch. I can't go on the computer and chat with the ladies (and one guy) on the Baby Days forum. I can't find out if *Eating 4 2* has had her baby or not (she went into early labor in the beginning of the week), and if it's a girl or a boy (she was the only one of us who didn't find out beforehand). I don't have a fork to eat with or a square of toilet paper to wipe with. The only thing left for my mother to pack into a box and tape up is me and the couch I'm stuck on. Oh, and the air conditioner—it's the beginning of autumn, but temps are still in the 80s. That does not make this pregnant woman very happy.

I ask my mother to check the mail five times before she gets exasperated with me and finally stomps downstairs. She returns with an armful of circulars and junk mail, depositing them on the couch next to me. I pick through the mail, not sure what I am looking for. I never put a return address or a name on my letter, so Julia wouldn't be able to respond directly to me, but somehow I'm expecting some sort of acknowledgement that she received my letter.

I've been scouring her column every day and there has been no mention of the Package Bandit. In fact, there has been no mention of him in the newspaper at all. There was a tiny blurb on the bottom of the last page in the community section on Tuesday simply stating that three houses in Dayville had packages stolen from their porches in the past week, but no mention on how it could be tied to the Package Bandit.

From these reports, it appears that Troy has moved on to Dayville—away from small businesses and onto the business of stealing from little old ladies. Of course, I have no way to know that the theft has only been of the elderly, but I can just see Troy sitting in his animal control van, twisting his villainous mustache and cackling as he watches a little old lady searching for a package on her front porch in vain. (Obviously this is an inaccurate portrayal of Troy since he doesn't have a mustache at all, but you get the point.)

I feel like I have already let the citizens of Dayville down. And I cannot let the citizens of my new town down like that...especially when I have the power to help. But I can't do anything on bedrest and I can't do anything here in this empty apartment.

I have no idea why Julia Heart hasn't taken action after receiving my letter. Unless...she didn't get my letter. I should call her to double check, but I can't even call her when my mother is out of earshot now because she has put the phone in a box and taped that up already. We are literally sitting here with nothing but a couch and some damn circulars.

On Saturday we are officially moving out of the apartment and into the new house. That's when I will finally have the opportunity to do some snooping in Dayville. That is, if I can get off of bedrest. For the good of the citizens of Dayville, (and my sanity) I *need* to get off of bedrest.

And I plan to do just that at my appointment on Saturday morning. Thankfully my mother is in the waiting room (after the hospital incident, Maria won't let her in the room anymore), so she can't hear me beg, but I actually *do* beg. If I thought I could get up, I would have gotten down on my knees to beg the doctor to release me from the prison of bedrest a week early.

Dr. Babin frowns and scratches his chin. "I'm not a fan of that idea Mrs. Maxwell. It's only seven more days. Isn't your baby's health worth seven more days of bedrest?"

Seven more days? Is that all he thinks is at stake here?

And that's when I completely lose it and start blubbering.

"The baby's health? The *baby's* health? What about *my* health? My *mental* health? I'm moving into a new house today and my mother packed all my stuff and my husband is stressed because he's working and painting and moving us into the house at the same time, pretty much on his own. And my sister stops by but she's no help at all, she's just passive aggressive talking about wine and hot tubs and all the things I'm not allowed to do. Did I mention that my mother has packed up all my stuff and watches me like I'm a prisoner looking to shiv another prisoner? I can't even get up to go get an envelope and a stamp to write a letter to the columnist who is going to solve the Package Bandit mystery. And that's driving me crazy because I know who's stealing the packages, but I can't talk about it with anyone, or my family will get mad at me for meddling and I can't call Carol because I can't find her cell phone number. And she doesn't like to walk my puppy—my mother, not Carol—but she's just a puppy and we don't have a fence at the new house yet because Roger forgot to set up the fence installation until it was too late to get it done before we move in so if she doesn't get walked at regular intervals she's going to pee all over the house and my mother will flip out. And don't tell me I should just relax and not think about all this! It's too hot to relax! Did I mention that my mother's packed everything up and I can't go on the computer because that's at the new house and it's not getting hooked up for a couple of days because of course that's not Roger's priority. I have no idea what's happening in my Baby Days chat room! I can't watch TV because we're not getting the cable installed until next week, so I can't even watch TV when we unpack the TV! I can't watch *A Baby Story* and I don't have anything to do because I read all the books I got from the library and I can't go and pick out more and I can't ask my mother to pick out books because she used to be an English lit major and she'll get me boring books like *Anna Karenia* when I really want to read Miss Marple. But I can't tell her to get me Miss Marple because I can't remember which Miss Marple books I've read. I actually have to see the book and read the blurb to remember if I read it. Oh, and my dad just got back to work because he was suspended because he got stung by a bee and hit a fireman's hearse and he wasn't drunk but they thought he was drunk and my mother had him to drive crazy. But now my mother doesn't have him to drive crazy all day every day so she is driving *me* crazy and I can't be on bedrest another day or I think I will lose my mind!"

Dr. Babin's eyes are the size of small saucers as he stares at me with grandfatherly concern. No doubt he is considering the fact that I have lost my mind already. Nothing I have said has made one iota of sense. It's not even in chronological order.

"Um, well Mrs. Maxwell, I can't actually advise you to, well, you know, go off of bedrest, but um…" he scratches his head and peers at me over his glasses. "I would say if I don't know what you're doing for the next seven days…at least don't lift any boxes or anything."

I could practically kiss the man as I catapult off the exam table. This nearly causes me to topple over, but I catch myself in time. Dr. Babin seriously looks frightened by me now.

"Thank you Dr. Babin!" I snatch up my purse, my mind working feverishly. I have five weeks' worth of snooping to catch up on. I'm not sure what to do first. Find Carol's number? Go down to the newspaper office and make sure that Julia got my letter? Follow Troy around in my car like a proper sleuth?

I am in such a fog, ideas and plans rolling around in my head that I don't even notice I have walked past my mother and father in the waiting room and I am now standing by their car in the parking lot. I am shaken from the fog by the sound of my mother's heels clicking on the pavement.

"Amy! What on earth are you doing, Amy?" By her voice, I can tell she's as irritated as an oyster with sand in it—except the only pearls I'll get from that irritation are my mother's "pearls of wisdom"...which I could do without right now.

"Sorry," I mumble, fiddling with the door handle. I hear my dad clicking the car open from behind me, near the entrance of the doctor's office. He's been very excited about this feature of his new car—he doesn't have to put the key in the lock and he can just open the door with a key fob. Technology fascinates him.

Both my mother and I climb into the overheated car and I briefly wish that my dad could not only open the car door from across the parking lot, but start the car as well. Obviously I realize that's impossible, but still, it would be nice, I think as I immediately stick to the leather seat like a window cling sticks to a window.

"You shouldn't be rushing around like that!" Mom admonishes as she dabs at her glistening forehead with a tissue. "You're on bedrest! You shouldn't be racing like you're a car in the Indy 500!"

"Oh, but I'm not!" I perk up, eager to share my good news. "Uh, Dr. Babin said I'm off of bedrest now!"

Mom is eying me warily. I offer a bright and cheery smile.

"What are you talking about, Amy?" Mom looks quite perturbed. "You're still on bed rest until next week!"

"But I'm not," I repeat happily. "Dr. Babin said I was free to go!"

I can tell my mother does not like—or believe—this.

"The doctor in the doctor in the hospital said you need to be on bed rest till 36 weeks. You're not 36 weeks yet." My mother sounds like a wailing siren. I don't understand why she's so put out by the idea of me not being on bedrest for another week. It certainly will free up *her* life—she won't have to babysit me all day now that I am allowed to get myself a glass of water and make my own grilled cheese sandwich.

I almost remind her of that, but she continues to complain before I can speak. "This is so irresponsible of that doctor," Mom says folding her arms angrily as Dad finally makes his way into the driver's seat, huffing and puffing as if he has run his first 5K.

"Jesus." He wipes away the beads of sweat on his upper lip. "You two racing or something?"

"Just drive," my mother orders, arms still crossed over her chest. "Drop Amy off first. She apparently doesn't *need* me anymore." She adds this last part with a snort.

My father nods as he continues to drive toward the apartment, but I remind him that the apartment is now empty and we need to go to the new house. Roger has asked a friend to help him move the couch to the house while I am at the doctor's. He has even brought the puppy to the new house. It's not ready completely ready, but the partially finished house is certainly better than the completely empty apartment.

My father pulls up to the house. "Doesn't look too bad. Can't believe you got this for so cheap. And in Dayville, no less."

"It could use a little TLC," I tell him as he rolls to a stop in our driveway, weeds growing out of the cracks in the asphalt.

"At least *someone* wants the TLC," my mother scoffs from the front seat, arms still planted against her chest.

That's when it dawns on me. She's ticked because she was enjoying being needed! That's why she was relishing my bedrest state—she *needs* to be needed!

Joey is well into her twenties, and Beth is also self-sufficient. When I was on bedrest, it was the first time my mother was needed in years. In the seventies, she quit her job as an English teacher to raise us and has never gone back to work, even after we went to school full time. She volunteered in the school library and was PTO president for a million years running. Even after we graduated high school, Mom didn't go and look for permanent work. She just joined garden clubs and went shopping every day. I had always assumed that's the way she had liked it. I never even suspected that she was lamenting the loss of being needed, and was desperately trying to fill up her time.

"Well, we're here." My father announces the obvious while stealing a glance at his watch. "I have a golf game in a bit, so we can't come in. I have to drop your mother off at home."

My mother makes a humphing noise from the front seat. I can swear she mutters something under her breath about not being needed again. I also swear I hear something along the lines of *I might as well just go and dig a hole and bury myself.*

Ugh! The guilt! The blasted mom guilt she's laying on me!

I get out of the car and rap my knuckles on her window. She frowns as she rolls the window down. "What?"

I cross one foot over the other in the driveway, experimenting with the art of actually standing on my own two feet...a novel concept for someone who has been on bedrest for weeks.

Taking a deep breath I say, "Listen, the doctor said I still can't be lifting anything right now. Even though I am *definitely* off bedrest." I make sure to point out the being off bedrest part. I don't need my mother marching back into the doctor's office and demanding to speak with the doctor or anything like that. I'm too close to freedom to allow that to happen.

"Uh huh," Mom says, lowering her sunglasses to peer at me. She is trying to act nonchalant, but I can tell that I have piqued her interest.

"So I could use some help still." I give her the most enthusiastic smile I can muster. I hear my father sigh with relief.

"Well," my mother says, pulling her purse over her shoulder. "I do have other things to do today, but I guess I can help out if you *really* need me to." She shoos me away from the door with her hand and opens it to step out onto the driveway. She slams the car door shut and leans into the window to speak with my father. "I'll call you when I'm done here."

I don't mention that our phone isn't hooked up yet and I don't have a cell phone and neither does she and Roger doesn't seem to be home at the moment. Instead, I just gaze at the house as my father pulls out of the driveway, flattening weeds underneath his tires. In my hand, I fiddle with the front door key absentmindedly and continue to stare at the house in disbelief. I can't believe it's ours.

"Come on, Amy," my mother clucks as she trots past me. She pushes aside the boxes stacked on the front porch—

labeled *Bathroom*—obviously dumped there by Roger this morning on his trip to the house. The computer and monitor appear to have been hidden behind it. Roger probably couldn't get the boxes *and* Misty *and* the computer in the house at the same time. In true Roger fashion, he probably forgot that he had left the computer on the front porch before he went back to the apartment for the rest of the boxes.

My mother pushes open the front door, muttering under her breath about how it's disgraceful that the door is unlocked and one never knows who is roaming the neighborhood looking to rifle through your things when you're not home even if the house doesn't have much in it to begin with.

I follow her inside the house in a daze. To my relief, the inside of the house is looking much more functional than I imagined. I can smell the fresh paint on the walls. Gazing around, I notice that the bright colors that I picked out make the house much more inviting. The stairway is almost glossy with a coat of sealant or something on it, and I absently wonder if the bottom step still creaks.

As Misty comes scrabbling out of the kitchen and enthusiastically leaps at me, I look down under my feet and notice that the hardwood floors have been sanded and sealed as well.

"Well these floors won't last long with that dog running around," my mother grumbles as she drops her purse down on the relocated couch that I had begun to think of as my home base over the past few weeks. I'm pretty sure the indent on the far right side is actually my butt imprint.

"Come on, Amy. Let's start in the most important room. We need to unpack the kitchen." Mom takes off, forgetting I can't move as fast as she can right now.

I waddle toward the kitchen like a newborn foal getting used to their legs, certain that my hipbones are going to fall out of their sockets. I rub them energetically as I enter the kitchen, discovering my mother poking at the boxes that are piled up on the kitchen table.

"Bloody men. Don't know how to unpack a house."

"What?" I ask, now rubbing at my back. I've been off of bedrest for less than an hour and I already want to go sit down on the couch. My body is betraying me with all these aches and pains.

My mother sweeps her hand over the collection of boxes on the table. "None of these boxes are for the kitchen, see?" She points to the side of one of the boxes, neatly labeled in her handwriting as *Linen Closet*. "These need to go upstairs in the bloody hallway to be unpacked into the linen closet," she says with disgust. I can tell she is super annoyed...she's speaking like a character in a bloody British novel. That's the extent of my mother's ability to curse...using the word *bloody* repeatedly.

"I bet the bloody kitchen stuff is parked near the bloody linen closet," she scoffs as she picks up the box and leaves the room with it in her arms.

"Where are you going?" I ask scurrying after her.

She spins and peers at me over the top of the box like I am dense. "I'm putting this box upstairs where it belongs and bringing the kitchen boxes down here. Really, Amy." She huffs and marches determinedly up the stairs. "Don't lift anything while I'm up here," she warns, her heels tapping each step and reverberating through the partially empty house.

"I won't," I call after her and briefly wonder if I should look through the rest of the boxes and make sure that none of them are for the kitchen and my mother didn't make a mistake. I decide that is probably not a good idea and wander off into the dining room instead.

Since we don't have a dining room table or chairs just yet, the boxes in this room are piled on the floor. I step into the room to take a look at them, not sure what boxes would have been dumped in a room that we have no furniture for yet.

Kitchen, the boxes all say.

I shake my head, not unlike the way my mother did when she discovered the linen closet boxes in the kitchen. I spread my legs wide so I can bend down to lift the box and bring it into the kitchen, when I remember that I'm not supposed to be lifting the boxes. I open my mouth to call upstairs to my mother (who I can hear stomping around, presumably looking for the kitchen boxes that are right here in the dining room), when a flash of white in front of the house catches my eye. I look out the window just as a white van slowly roll by, as if the driver is looking for something. A chill creeps up my body as I see the letters on the side say *Animal Control*. Misty, besides me, lets out a low growl as the van stops in front of our house.

I realize I'm holding my breath and I let out a long exhale as Troy climbs out of the front seat of the van and glances around. There are no cars in the driveway, so from his standpoint, there doesn't appear to be anyone home. I can't imagine why he would stop here, until I realize that the computer and boxes piled up on the front porch have attracted his attention. He quickly scoots up the front walk and Misty begins to yelp excitedly.

"Shhh, Misty," I admonish as I tuck myself into the corner of the dining room, out of his sight. His muscular arms are still visible from my vantage point as they wrap themselves around the computer on our front porch. Those arms lift it, carry it down the stairs, and place it into the back of the animal control van.

Even from the corner of the dining room, I can see Troy looking around again, assuring himself that he has not been seen, before climbing into the van. As he drives away, I think, *He just stole my computer off my front porch. I should do something about that.* Still, I'm frozen, rooted to the spot with shock.

"Amy! What on earth are you doing? Why are you hiding in the corner?"

My mother's voice startles me out of my shocked state.

"Um, I just found these kitchen boxes here," I stammer, tapping at the cardboard boxes with my foot.

"And when were you going to tell me that, Amy? After I was done tearing apart the entire second floor in search of these boxes?" She sighs in a manner that I became very accustomed to as a child—my mother was often annoyed with my lack of what she called "common sense". I can only assume that not immediately alerting her to the kitchen box situation was once again considered lacking in the aforementioned "common sense".

"Sorry. I got distracted," I tell her. And it's true. I did get distracted. But I immediately regret my words. My mother is nosy—she's going to want to know *what* distracted me. I cannot possibly tell her I got distracted by the fact that my co-worker just stole a computer off my front porch, and that I'm pretty sure he's the Package Bandit that they've been talking about in the paper. She would certainly start ranting about alerting the police, considering, that's what "common sense" would dictate.

And as we all know, my pregnant brain is not operating under the standard umbrella of the usual common sense that is gifted to non-pregnant people. My pregnant brain does not even consider the option of calling the police at all. My pregnant brain is determined to catch Troy myself. But I won't be able to do that if my mother snoops in.

Thankfully, Misty sees to it that my mother barely hears what I've said by continuing to yelp uncontrollably.

"What on earth has gotten into that dog?" My mother shakes her head at Misty who is literally leaping all over the dining room as she barks. When I notice Misty's leash is hanging on a hook by the front door, an idea forms in my slow-witted pregnant brain. Once again, I'm going to use the puppy as a means to escape from the house.

"She needs to go for a walk," I say.

"So let her out in the yard," my mother says with a dismissive wave of her hand.

"But we don't have the fence yet! The fence isn't being installed for a few weeks! I have to walk her on the leash." For once I am happy that it took Roger so long to call the fence company. They were all booked up till November by the time he contacted them.

My mother sighs heavily as she leans over and picks up a kitchen box. "Well, don't take too long. I could use help unpacking this box." She sashays off toward the kitchen, heels clicking on the newly refinished floor. I swear I have no idea how she still has those shoes on. I would be in flip flops by now.

I glance down at my feet. I *am* in flip flops, even though it's October. My feet are so swollen that I can't even fathom the idea of trying to stuff them into a pair of shoes.

I grab Misty's leash before wasting another minute contemplating my mother's footwear selections. Misty dances excitedly as I attempt several times to snap on the leash. I bet she is eager to explore her new neighborhood. I am eager to catch the thief in her new neighborhood.

I open the front door and she yanks me through the opening. I am barely able to register the fact that yes indeed, the computer is gone, before the puppy is pulling me down the stairs of the front porch and to the walkway. "Slow down, girl! Mommy hasn't gone for a walk in a while!"

Misty ignores me as she pulls me down the sidewalk, face to the ground, sniffing as if she is hot on the scent of something. Who knows, maybe she is. Maybe she can track Troy and his animal control van. I am practically jogging to keep up with her, my legs creaking, my belly heavy, my milk-filled boobs jiggling all over the place. That reminds me that I have to ask a question about the milk leaking on the Baby Days forum. *Why are they leaking already? Is that normal?*

Then I remember that I don't have a freaking computer and it's Troy's fault. My anger swells. *I need to catch that van!*

Misty abruptly turns when we reach the first corner, her short little puppy legs moving so feverishly that they're like a blur in front of me. She is definitely tracking something. If not Troy, a rogue squirrel or another dog. "Misty, please slow down," I pant, cupping the underside of my belly with my free hand.

And just like that, Misty does stop. Right in front of the van with *Animal Control* written on the side. I gasp, looking around for Troy, but don't see him anywhere. I peer toward the house the van is parked in front of, wondering if he has gone around the back to steal another package. He's not on the back porch, though...I can see it from where I stand.

I place my shaking hand on the back of the van. My computer is back here. I saw him put my computer in this very van.

If I could just get the door open, I think, fingers gripping the handle. *Maybe I'll need to...*

Without any effort at all, the back door of the van swings open. I gasp again as I peek inside, certain that I will see boxes and our computer.

Instead, I am shocked to discover that the back of the van is empty.

"What the hell are you doing?"

I spin on my heel, my heart hammering in my chest. Troy is standing right next to me, glowering, hands clenched at his sides like he's going to knock me out. Misty's lip has curled into a snarl and she's emitting a very low growl. She attempts to lunge at Troy and he falters for a second, backing up.

"Um, hi, Troy," I stammer.

"What are you doing in my van?" he says slowly, the way one might when speaking to a person who doesn't understand English, as if they will get what you're saying if you talk slower.

"I was just—"

Misty stops growling and is full on barking now.

"Will you shut that mutt up?" Troy snarls, swinging his size 12 boot out at her head. Fortunately he misses, but I can tell from the ire on his face that if he kicks again, he'll make a point not to miss.

"I'm sorry," I say, attempting to sound contrite while fudging my story a bit. "It's just that our computer was stolen off our front porch a little while ago, and the um, well, the *neighbor* said that a white van had been in front of the house. So um, I saw your van and thought that maybe—"

"That *I* stole your computer," Troy says with a laugh. "Why would I be stealing computers off people's porches? I don't do stuff like that."

He stares at me, an incredulous expression on his face. It's very convincing. If I hadn't seen him take the computer with my own two eyes, I would have thought he really didn't take it.

"Like I said, I—"

"I have to go," Troy snaps, pushing past me, but avoiding Misty's tiny snapping teeth. He yanks open the driver's side door and climbs in, slamming it shut behind him. Misty and I jump out of the way as exhaust pours from the tailpipe and Troy roars off, leaving us staring after him.

Crap. Where did he put my computer?

8.5

Bun in the Oven: *Has anyone heard from Maxwell Mommy?*

Mum 2B: *Not for a few weeks now. That's weird. She used to post at least once a week.*

Bun in the Oven: *I hope everything is okay, With Eating 4 2 going into early labor with her son and all that.*

George's Gal: *Didn't Mom to 3 go into labor early, too?*

Mum 2B: I think so.

Bun in the Oven: *I hope Maxwell Mommy didn't go into labor. She was on bedrest, right?*

Mum 2B: *Maxwell Mommy's due soon enough. I think she's 36 or 37 weeks now.*

Mom to 3: *Yes, just like me. I was 36 weeks when I gave birth to Rory. He's such a joy! However, it is best to get as close to 40 weeks as possible for the health of the baby.*

Mum 2B: *Welcome back Mom to 3! Congrats on Rory's birth!*

Bun in the Oven: *Yah! So happy for you!*

Mom to 3: *Thank you! We just got home yesterday. It's been quite a challenge going from 3 kids to 4.*

George's Gal: *Congrats! Will you be changing your screen name to Mom to 4?*

Mom to 3: *I really haven't had time to think about that.*

In a Baby Daze: *I know why Maxwell Mommy hasn't been on. She's probably sick of this group and their stupid questions. That's a stupid question George's Gal.*

Mom to 3: *If you don't have anything nice to say, don't say anything at all, In a Baby Daze!*
Bun in the Oven: *She'd be totally mute then!*

****

Roger is nearly beside himself about the computer being stolen off the front porch. He can't believe that neither me, nor my mother, saw anyone take it. He calls the police, of course, but they simply shrug and file the report, while insinuating that Roger must be some kind of a moron for leaving his computer on the front porch where someone can just come along and take it.

Doesn't he read the paper? Listen to the news? There's a package thief on the loose. Only a complete idiot would leave something as tempting as a computer on the front porch. My mother suggests more of the same after the police leave. I just keep my mouth shut.

Yes, yes, I know. I should tell the police what I know. But without the computer in Troy's possession, it's just his word against mine. And I don't want to tip him off to the fact that I'm on to him by alerting the police.

I'm going to just have to keep my fingers crossed and hope that Julia Heart has taken my letter seriously, and is investigating the package bandit and the lead I have given her. It's probably best that she takes care of it anyway. She's completely mobile and doesn't have a giant pregnant belly weighing her down. *And* she has a working computer, I'm sure, something I am lacking at the moment.

Of course, now that don't have a computer, I have no way of checking into the Baby Days forum, either. It's the middle of October now and everyone in my October baby group is going to be giving birth soon. I feel completely out of the loop without access to the internet. I have nothing else to do but unpack the house.

I'm unpacking some dishes in the kitchen when the phone rings on the wall.

"Amy!" The voice on the other end is not asking, it's telling. I'm not exactly sure who it is until she snaps, "This is Amanda."

Ah, Amanda. I haven't had the pleasure of speaking to her since before the day I passed out at the hospital, more than six weeks ago. When I called the animal shelter to say I wouldn't be back until after the baby was born, Bridget had answered the phone. She had been sad at the prospect of not seeing me at work, but she reminded me that my health and the baby's health was of utmost importance. She had even sent me a "Get well/Good luck" card in the mail, with a Babies R Us gift card in it. I was so thrilled, and I called to thank her, but Amanda had answered so I slammed down the phone. I told myself that I would call back on a Tuesday, Amanda's day off, but apparently my preggo brain completely forgot to do that.

"Hello, Amanda," I try to say as kindly as one can speak to their arch nemesis.

"Amy, your final check got mailed back to us. Did you move or something?"

"Oh, um, yeah. We moved a few weeks ago."

"Well, it came back with no forwarding address. Why didn't you go to the post office and register a forwarding address? Don't you know you're supposed to register a forwarding address when you move?" she asks accusingly.

My face warms and despite the fact that it is only fifty-four degrees this morning, I am flushed. How dare she accuse me of being stupid! Okay, maybe she didn't exactly call me *stupid*, but she certainly implied that I was stupid for not updating the post office with a forwarding address.

"I thought I did," I mumble.

"Well, come and pick it up today. Bridget wants to talk to you about your *job*, too." She says this with such an air of smugness that I wonder for a second if my job is in jeopardy or something.

Maybe Bridget is mad I didn't tell her about the baby after all? No, that makes no sense! She sent me a gift!

I glance at the kitchen clock. I have a doctor's appointment at one o'clock, and it's eleven o'clock now. Surely I have enough time to get over to the animal shelter and back by then. Plus, if I go to the animal shelter, maybe I'll be able to do a little digging on Troy.

"Sure," I tell Amanda. I hang up the phone and grab my jacket. It's not like I have anything better to do.

****

I arrive at the animal shelter and find the parking lot is deserted except for Bridget and Amanda's cars. I don't see Troy's animal control van anywhere. I am slightly disappointed, but then I remember what happened the last time I saw Troy and I shudder. I don't want to have to see him again. At least if he's not around, I can suggest to Bridget that she should look in the back of the van sometime.

Yes! That's perfect! I'll hand this off to Bridget! She'll know what to do!

Armed with a plan, I enter the animal shelter and the bell above the door jingles. Amanda looks up from the computer and scowls when she sees that it's me. Without a word, she reaches under the desk and retrieves an envelope which she holds out to me. I step up to the counter and take it from her outstretched hand.

"Thanks," I say with a nod of my head.

"Stay there," is all she says as she turns and heads toward the back room. I assume she is going to let Bridget know that I am here.

I lean my elbow on the counter as I wait for them to return, contemplating what I should say to Bridget.

Should I tell her about my computer being stolen or should I just mention the packages I saw in the van?

I glance at the computer while thinking, and the blinking cursor on the computer screen gives me an idea. *Hey! Maybe I can check into the Baby Days forum while I'm here.*

Peeking down the hall to make sure that Amanda isn't on her way back yet, I duck behind the counter and click the mouse over the internet browser button. I quickly type in the address for Baby Day and click the November Babies link.

I quickly scroll down and discover that Eating 4 2 and Mom of 3 have both given birth. Both to boys. A few people have asked about me and my heart swells with joy. *They missed me!*

I am about to type a response to one of the questions about my whereabouts when I hear Amanda's screechy voice.

"Just what do you think you're doing?"

I spin around, guilt written all over my face. "Sorry, Amanda, I just needed to use the computer really quickly. Ours was—"

"You have no right to use my computer!" Amanda speeds toward me, finger poking the air accusingly.

"Well, I mean, I just figured since I work here I—"

"Ha!" Amanda retorts with a villainous smile. "We'll see about that!"

"What is *that* supposed to mean?"

"Go see Bridget and you'll find out." She points toward Bridget's office. There is no confusion about the smugness in Amanda's voice this time.

I stare at her pointing finger but don't respond. Instead, I just stick my chin out in the air in a defiant manner and stomp off toward Bridget's office—as best as a pregnant woman can storm off—like a kid being sent to the principal's office. My legs are shaking like Jello.

I have no idea why I'm nervous. *I* haven't done anything wrong. *I'm* not the one who's involved in illegal activity. *I* haven't stolen packages from little old ladies. *I* am certainly not the one who stole my computer off my front porch. If anyone should be nervous, it should be Troy. Not that he's here or anything, but I'm not the one who's been bad. Justice is about to be served.

As I approach Bridget's office I can see her hunched over the account books. She's always doing this—apparently the animal shelter isn't very well funded, so she's constantly trying to get blood from a stone. Or so she says. She must sense that I'm standing behind her because she swivels in her chair and faces me.

"Amy!" She starts to smile, but the grin quickly fades. "Um, hi. Come in. Have a seat." She waves her hand toward the chair in the corner. There is a hefty bag of dog food on top of it. "Let me grab that," she says, bounding to her feet and pulling the bag to the floor so I can sit.

"Thanks." I take a seat, tucking my legs to the side since the bag of dog food is still sort of in my way, taking up room in front of the chair.

Bridget offers me a weak smile as she sits back down in her own chair. I've never seen Bridget as anything less than one hundred percent confident, but I notice she's actually twisting up the bottom of her sweater into her hands and not looking me in the eye. "Um, Amy. I have something that I need to tell you."

"I have something I have to tell you as well. It's about Troy."

Bridget looks taken aback by my revelation. "Oh. So you know about this?"

I cock my head to the side. *Of course I know about this! How does she know about this?* "Wait...*you* know about Troy?"

Bridget nods. "He's the one who told us."

Perplexed, I ask, "He *told* you? What did he tell you exactly?"

"Listen, Amy, there's really no easy way to say this." She cringes as if this conversation is actually causing her pain as she continues to twist her sweater, stretching it out.

"Well, um, just say it, I guess." I have no idea what she's about to say.

"I..." Just then, Amanda walks into the office.

"Gotta get something from the um, files," she says, but by the way she's leaning in toward us, I can tell she's just trying to eavesdrop on the conversation.

Bridget ignores her and continues to try to speak. "I, well, it's not my decision, you see—"

"*What's* not your decision?" I ask. *What on earth does this have to do with Troy stealing packages?*

Amanda sighs and whirls around, file folder in hand.

"You're fired," Amanda announces with gusto.

"Amanda!" Bridget cries with anguish.

"What?" Amanda shrugs. "You weren't doing it!"

"Wait...*what*? Why would *I* be fired? Troy is the one stealing packages!"

Bridget wrinkles her brow. "Stealing packages? What are you talking about, Amy?"

"What are *you* talking about?" I'm suddenly not so certain that justice is about to be served anymore.

"Troy's not *stealing* anything!" Amanda says haughtily.

Bridget ignores Amanda and starts rubbing her temples. "Troy told us about seeing you in Dayville."

"Yes. I saw him a few weeks ago. He's the one who's been—"

"He said he saw you kick the puppy that you adopted from the shelter," Amanda says, crossing her arms over her chest.

It's like someone has sucker punched me in my ginormous abdomen and then drained all the air from the room. "What?" I manage to gasp. "He's the one who—" I can't even finish the sentence.

"The puppy that you shouldn't have even gotten," Amanda adds.

"What do you mean by *that*?" Although, I think I know *exactly* what she means by that.

"After he told us about this, um, incident, Amanda did some research." Bridget says *research*, but somehow, it sounds like what she means is *snooping*. "It turns out that the family that wanted to adopt the puppy didn't call and say they're not interested. Apparently someone from here called and told them that the puppy's owner had come for her. And then the same day, you decided to take the puppy home."

I slink down in the seat. Okay, I definitely didn't hurt the puppy, but the second part of this story is true. Still, it doesn't seem like a reason to fire a person.

"So given all the circumstances, the board has decided that it's just best to let you go." Bridget bows her head. "I'm sorry. It's really out of my hands."

"But, Bridget, Troy is the person stealing the packages!"

She wrinkles up her nose. "You said that. What packages?"

"The packages being stolen around town. You know, by the Package Bandit?"

Bridget sighs. "Amy—"

"Troy is the Package Bandit!" I push myself out of the chair and practically topple over the bag of dog food on the floor. "In fact, he even stole my computer from my front porch! I saw him with my own two eyes!"

"Why are you making up lies about him?" Amanda is glowering at me. "You're being confronted with the things *you* did and now you're making up stuff, trying to get him in trouble? Wow. That's low. Even for you. Face it. You don't belong here. You *never* belonged here. You've done some crappy things and now you're trying to make Troy look bad."

"Amanda—" Bridget is now feverishly rubbing her temples. She closes her eyes as if she could make both of us disappear.

"I am not the one who—"

I stop talking because Amanda is hovering over me. And she's a heck of a lot bigger than I am. Even at eight and a half months pregnant, Amanda's got twenty pounds and five inches on me. At least. I am not getting into this with her. I don't put it past her to punch me or at the very least, slap me.

"If you don't believe me, I'm going to the police."

I push past her and race to the front door, tears swimming in my eyes. I fumble blindly out the door and into the sunshine, which blinds me even further. I dig in my purse for my keys. Hands trembling, I open the car door and slide into the driver's seat. Because of my shaking hands, it takes me three attempts to stick the key in the ignition and get the car to start. Tears have spilled over my eyelids and are running down my face.

I can't believe that I'm losing my job because Troy has completely turned the tables and lied about me!

He probably assumed (correctly) that I was going to try to rat him out to Bridget or the police, after our confrontation on the street. Then I bet he got Amanda to dig up dirt about the puppy to make me look even worse! She'd do anything he asked without question. And Troy's going to get away with it because no one will believe me! It's my word against his—and now I look like a liar because of how I sabotaged the puppy's adoption. *Why didn't I go to the police when I had the chance?*

I wipe away my tears and take a deep breath. It's after noon now. I only have about forty-five minutes or so to get to my doctor's appointment. Forty-five minutes to go to the police, and that is the most important thing right now. I cannot drive this car if I'm hysterically crying.

Gripping the steering wheel with both hands, I inhale sharply and pull out of the parking lot. I turn the corner behind the building, heading in the direction of the police station.

That is, until someone leaving the back of the building catches my eye. I blink twice, sure I am mistaken, but no. It's Troy and he's headed toward the animal control van parked behind the building. I didn't notice it when I pulled into the parking lot because it's not in its usual spot. A clammy sensation shudders over me as I realize something.

Troy must have been in the building the whole time I was talking to Bridget. He heard what I said to her. He knows I'm planning to go to the police. I bet he's going to make sure he gets rid of all the evidence now.

Quickly pulling over to the side of the road, I watch in the rearview mirror as Troy speeds out of the parking lot, turning down the road I'm stopped on. He passes my car, with no indication that he recognizes it.

Stealthily, I pull in traffic behind him, keeping my distance. My heart is hammering so loudly in my chest that I turn up the volume on the radio hoping to drown out the sound. It doesn't work—it's still pulsing loudly in my ears, the swishing blood pounding out a mantra: *Just go to the police, Amy, just go to the police.*

I ignore the mantra and tail the van, now going in the opposite direction of my doctor's office. If I continue to follow him, I'm definitely going to be late for my appointment. There will be no time to turn around. *Turn around, turn around,* the heartbeat is telling me, but I dismiss it.

We pass the police station, and now the sound in my head switches back to *go to the police, go to the police.* Ignoring it, I see Troy peek in his side mirror and I lower my head, hoping he hasn't spotted me. He doesn't speed up or turn or do anything suspicious, so I assume he hasn't seen me.

Still, I'm not going to take any chances—I let a car get in between us, just to be on the safe side. Oddly enough, it seems like Troy is headed toward Dayville, toward our new house. A wave of fear pulses through me.

What if he's going to exact his revenge on me somehow? Come to the house? Try to steal something else? Or kidnap *me?* I try shake off the thoughts with logic. *Don't be silly, Amy. He's a package thief, not a kidnapper.*

Regardless, this does nothing to slow my racing heart. It definitely doesn't help that Troy is taking the exact route I would have taken back to my house had I been planning to go there instead of the doctor's office or the police station.

We turn onto my street and my left leg starts trembling involuntarily, calf muscle choosing that exact moment to lock up in a Charley Horse. I try to massage the back of my calf on the car seat as Troy slows down in front of my house, but to my relief, he bypasses it and turns down the next block. The van stops in front of the very same house I found him at on the day our confrontation.

Is he stealing something else from this house?

I drive past—I can't very well stop and let him see my car, can I? I pull onto the next block and park my car in front of the first house, a brick ranch, completely out of Troy's sight. As I rub my sore calf, begging it to cooperate, I notice that this street is on the route Roger takes to get to our house from the school. Thank goodness he won't be getting out of work for another few hours then.

Still shaking, I swing the car door open. My back spasms as I haul my roly-poly body out of the car and walk back toward the van. My calf is screaming as well. I cringe, but otherwise ignore the pain. It seems to dissipate as I walk anyway.

There are hedges on the corner, perfect for hiding behind as I peek out and spy on Troy. I see him at the back of the van, removing a stack of boxes. He carries them toward the house.

Son of a bitch! He's not stealing from this house...he's dropping things off here!

I can't see him anymore from behind the bush, so I sneak out and creep up the sidewalk until he's in my sight again. He's at the back of the house, at the garage. He knocks on the door of the garage and it opens. I can't get a good look at the person who opens the door—they're in the shadows and Troy ducks inside too quickly, closing the door behind him.

I must see what he's doing in there and who he's with, I decide, ignoring that nagging part of my brain that's telling me to get back in the car and go to the police. Or at the very least, go to my doctor's appointment like a good pregnant woman.

I scurry up the driveway and slink along the side of the garage. Well, I scurry and slink as much as one can when one is eight and a half months pregnant. I press my back against the fence along the side of the garage, trying to blend in with the surroundings, aka. shrubbery. In the process, I manage to tweak the muscle in my back again. This time the pain radiates around my entire midsection. I rub it feverishly with my hand—what an inconvenient time for back pain.

After a minute or so, the rubbing seems to help and I'm able to continue my mission. I notice that there is a small window at the back of the garage, and I thank heaven for the fact that bush is growing right in front of it. I can hide next to the bush and still see into the garage. I impatiently push the bush aside so I can slip next to it. I want to get this over with as soon as possible because I have just felt pressure on my bladder. That can only mean one thing. I have to pee.

Crouching down as much as one can crouch down when one is eight and a half months pregnant, having back pain, and needs to pee, I peer into the garage window. I have to bite my lip to prevent myself from gasping at what lies before me.

In the garage there are shelving units against every wall. On those shelving units are packages. Many, many, *many* packages. Some are open and some are still sealed shut. There is a stack of empty boxes in the corner of the garage, packing tape on the floor next to them. In the middle of the garage sits a card table, extension cords snaking to the far corner of the garage and into an outlet. On top of the card table sits a computer and a printer. *My computer, maybe?* I can't tell from here. Stacks of opened boxes and piles of newspaper lie next to the card table. Next to the stacks, a guy with a face of a weasel is taping up boxes. *Rodney! He must be in on this with Troy!*

While Rodney boxes things up, Troy sits at the card table on a folding chair, his back to me, entering information into the computer. I can't make out exactly what he's typing, but it looks like some sort of spreadsheet. Bridget uses them at the animal shelter to keep track of donations and expenditures. I highly doubt that's what Troy is keeping track of though. More like he's cataloguing the stolen goods from the packages. My guess is he and Rodney are selling them as well.

Troy opens another window and types in more information. Then he presses a button and the printer whirls to life. After removing a piece of paper from the printer, Troy hands the paper to Rodney who immediately gets busy affixing it to a box with some more packing tape. He drops the box in another pile by the garage door.

They repeat this process several times over the course of the next half hour or so—Troy printing, Rodney packing and taping. I wish that I had my camera with me so that I could take a picture before all this evidence disappears. I don't know how I'm going to prove anything to the police. *The spreadsheet? The computer?* I'm not tech savvy, so I would have no idea if the police could retrieve the spread sheet or anything Troy has printed.

I've got to figure out what to do soon, though. Despite my efforts to remain immobile (or maybe because of them), my back is still bothering me, cramping up on and off, and my desire to go to the bathroom has not abated at all. In fact, it's getting worse by the second.

The window of the garage is cracked and dust motes dance out into the early fall afternoon. A few of them find their way up my nose, tickling the inside. I quickly cover my entire nose and mouth with my hand, a sneeze building.

Please don't sneeze, please don't sneeze, I beg myself. I can just see the headlines now: *Woman Killed by Package Bandit When a Sneeze Gives Her Away.*

I can't stifle the sneeze, but I manage to contain it and not make a sound. Unfortunately, my bladder has not been able to withstand the pressure of the sneeze. I immediately feel a trickle down the leg of my sweatpants.

Damn it!

Torn between watching Troy and Rodney and the desire to change my pants, I ultimately decide to change my pants. I start to creep back down the side of the garage toward the driveway, rationalizing that if I go home to change my pants, I can grab my camera and take pictures of the garage before they have a chance to get rid of all of this stuff.

I am almost to the edge of the driveway when I hear the garage door creak open. Flattening myself against the fence (or as much as one can flatten oneself when one is eight and a half months pregnant), I try to remain absolutely still and not make any noise. Troy is carrying an armful of the packages that he just boxed up. He doesn't see me as he heads to the van and opens the back, shoving the packages inside. He slams the door shut and jogs back toward the garage, presumably to retrieve more items.

Despite my rather moist sweatpants, back pain, racing heart, and the nagging feeling that I should go home and get my camera and call the police, I speed walk toward the van. In the street I am out of sight of the garage, so I quietly pull the back door open and climb inside, closing the door at the speed of pudding to prevent it from slamming. Because there are no windows in this part of the van, it's much darker in here than I anticipated. Fumbling in the darkness, I nearly trip over the packages that Troy has just placed inside the van. I try to read the name and address on top of the first package, but it's impossible to see in this lighting. Even though I can't read the writing, a familiar primary color logo catches my eye.

He's selling this stuff in an online marketplace!

I pick up the package in both hands—it's pretty heavy—and trudge over to the front of the van where light is streaming in from the windshield. As I do that, a shadow passes over me and I realize that Troy is walking toward the van!

I lower my aching and heavy body to the floor of the van, just as I hear his key in the driver's door. It creaks open and he drops into the seat. The key turns in the ignition and the van roars to life. I press my body against the wall of the van, along the animal cages, my brain and heart racing as he pulls away from the curb.

I'm trapped in the van with Troy! He's going to find out I'm in here when he stops to retrieve the packages to mail! He's going to kill me! Why didn't I just go to the police?

All of those thoughts are overshadowed by the sudden and intense pain that rocks my body at that moment. It is then that I realize that I did not pull a back muscle and I did not pee my pants when I sneezed.

Crap. I'm in labor.

9

You are 9 months pregnant! Congratulations! You've made it to the end of your pregnancy! This baby is coming sooner rather than later! It's been a long 9 months and maybe you are anxiously waiting for labor to begin. Perhaps you are looking for ways to speed it up such as by using laxatives or eating spicy foods. Don't! Any attempts to hasten labor may increase the likelihood that you'll need medical intervention during labor (ie. C-section). It'll happen soon enough—don't worry. Hopefully you have prepared for your delivery by taking a child-birthing class. While that's helpful, remember that labor and delivery is an extremely personalized experience. No two women experience it exactly the same way, so try to put your expectations and fears aside.

There are common signs that you're in labor. You may notice cramping—several minutes apart and with a consistent duration. (Time them if you're not sure!) Your water may break (although only 10% of women report spontaneous breaking of their water as their first sign of labor—this usually needs to be done in the hospital or happens as labor progresses). Back pain and nausea are also common symptoms of labor. Bloody show and losing your mucus plug are also signs that you're ready to deliver.

Be sure to call your doctor as soon as you can. They will advise you on the best time to go to the hospital. While you don't want to get there too early, you don't want to have the baby on the way there, either! Good luck! You're going to need it!

****

Oh my God! This is nuts! An insane amount of pain! I really think this kind of pain should come with some sort of warning. Did they warn me it would hurt this *much in that class? Or all those books I read? I think not. And Mom didn't warn me about this either! I have a few choice words for* her *when I'm done with this, that's for sure.*

I know they said it was painful, but my God! They could have mentioned I was going to feel like an antelope being torn apart by a hungry mountain lion. It's like I'm being split in half!

Okay…it's stopped for a second. Take a deep breath.

I guess Beth was right when she said I wasn't ready to be a mother. Ugh! Why didn't I listen? Well, not that there was anything I could have done about it at that point…

Why didn't I listen to the doctor and take it easy? It's too early! I'm not supposed to have this baby for another three weeks! If I had listened to the doctor this wouldn't be happening.

Wait! Is there some way to stop this kid from coming out? Or maybe someone can just cut me open and take it out? I know I said I wanted to do the whole natural labor thing and all, but I've changed my mind!

Oh wait, I have no choice. I have to do this natural labor thing no matter what! Get down on all fours, Amy, and rock. Didn't that labor coach, midwife lady tell you that would help with the pain? Do it now, before the pain starts to build again. These contractions are like a minute apart. It can't be too long now.

How did I get in this situation? Well, I know how I got into the whole being pregnant *situation, thank you very much! What I mean is, how did I get into* this *situation...giving birth...*here. *Is that a bag of dog poop over in the corner? Oh, this can't be very sanitary.*

Beth will faint dead away when I tell her about this. She would want to give birth in a pool of sea water with tinkling music playing in the background while a masseuse rubs her shoulders. Hey, that actually doesn't sound too bad right—

Here comes the pain again! Breathe, Amy! Breathe! This sucks that I have to remind myself to breathe! That should be Roger's job. Roger should be reminding me to breathe. I miss Roger! I wish he was here. I want Roger! I need Roger!

Oh my God, I'm going to scream. No, I can't scream! Bite your tongue, Amy! Or your lip. Just bite something. If you scream, he's going to know you're in here. And then *what are you going to do? How are you going to explain being in the back of a dog catcher's van, down on all fours, giving birth?*

Crap. I'm going to scream.

I do just that and my body lurches forward. Troy slams on the breaks. He sticks his head in between the front seat and the back of the van, eyes bulging out of his head.

"What the hell are you doing back there?" he yells, his face frantic.

"What does it look like I'm doing back here? Serving tea to the Queen? I'm having a baby, you idiot!"

In retrospect, I realize it's probably not a good idea to call the driver of the animal control van that you have snuck onto and are currently in labor in, an idiot. However, I am obviously not thinking too clearly at this time, being in labor and all.

"No, what are you doing back *there*? Why are you in my van?"

"I don't have time to explain," I pant, screwing up my eyes against the pain. "I'm *literally* having the baby right now! Take me to the hospital!"

The van doesn't move and I open my eyes to see Troy thoughtfully scratching his chin as he looks at me.

"What are you waiting for?" I scream at him. "Drive the damn van to the hospital!"

Troy stands up and squeezes between the front seats. He's standing in the entrance to the back of the van, a mere three feet from where I am. He glares down at me, stroking his chin, like a mobster in a mob movie.

"What, what are you doing?" I stammer. A contraction starts up, sucking the air out of the van and I am unable to speak as he takes another step toward me in what can only be described as a menacing manner. I want to shuffle backward on my rear, closer to the back of the van, but the contraction has me paralyzed.

"So you think you can spy on me, try to get me fired, sneak into the back of my van, and I'm just going to do what you ask me to do?" he finally says after what feels like an eternity of silence.

He continues to stare at me, as if he's waiting for an answer. "Well?" he barks.

"Oh, um, I thought it was a rhetorical—" I suck in my breath, the next contraction sneaking up like a ninja. "Oh shit," I gasp, a ripping sensation exploding in my crotch.

"Oh shit what?" Troy asks, bad guy expression chased off his face. "Oh shit *what*?"

"I think," I pant, my fingers trembling as I run my hand to crotch portion of my sweatpants. "I think I feel the head. I think the baby is coming right now!"

"What?" Troy's bad guy persona is now *completely* gone, and in its place is a panic-stricken animal control officer who looks like a rabid raccoon is flailing toward his face. "You can't have a baby in here!"

"Didn't...didn't they teach you how to deliver a...oh my god!" I wail.

"I don't know how to deliver a baby!" Troy slaps his hands over his face.

"Well, someone has to deliver this baby and I'm a little busy here!"

Troy shakes his head. "Stay...stay here!" As if I had a choice in the matter. He squeezes back between the seats and starts up the van. "Just don't...don't *push*!"

Just then, I hear a tapping on the window. Crap! Rodney! I forgot about him! Troy may not be a total bad guy, but I'm pretty sure Rodney is. If Rodney finds me in the back of the van, who knows what'll happen.

Troy awkwardly leans across the seats and rolls down the window. My body shakes. I'm not sure if it's from the contractions or what Troy is going to say to Rodney. "I've got—"

"Drop this one off, too," Rodney says, dumping a package on the front seat. He doesn't even notice me in the back. Troy stares at the package and then back at Rodney (I assume he's walking back to the garage) as if in a trance.

Another contraction hits and I roar, "Get me to the mother freaking hospital, Troy!"

Troy startles and shakes his head. "Yes, yes. The hospital."

He screeches away from the curb and bump through the streets, toward the hospital...I hope. Troy is shouting things like *don't push* and *almost there* and *I don't know how to cut the cord.*

The contractions are stacking up one on top of the other, coming so quickly now that I have no time to recover in between. I feel like my pelvis is split in two and I am really starting to believe that I am indeed going to give birth in the back of this animal control van. And quite honestly at this point in time, I don't even care. I just want this baby out. She is literally killing me right now.

The van screeches to a halt. Troy leaps from the driver's seat, leaving the door open. I hear his footfalls as he runs around the side of the van and the back doors fly open.

"She's in labor! She's in labor!" Troy is crying out. "Somebody help!" He is jumping up and down and waving his hands around like he's trying to flag down a taxi.

"You can't park here, sir," I hear a woman say. "We don't take animals here. This is a people hospital."

"I *know* that! I have a human mother here giving birth!" Troy snaps.

"In the back of a dog catcher's van?"

"I'm an animal control officer, damn it!"

A face peers around the back door of the van and the eyes belonging to that face widen at the sight of me—spread eagle leaning against the cages, panting. The face confirms that I am indeed a human and in labor.

"My goodness, ma'am!" The woman turns and calls to someone behind her, "Get a wheelchair!" The woman, who is wearing a security guard uniform, reaches her hand out to me, but I can't move. I seriously, honest to goodness, cannot drag my body to the edge of the van to get out. Someone is going to have to carry me out of this van, damn it.

"We can't do that, ma'am," the woman says. I am confused until I realize that I must have said that out loud. Oh well. At this point I really can't be responsible for what I say out loud, can I?

"Get a doctor," the security guard says to someone over her shoulder as she heaves herself into the back of the van. Out of the corner of my eye, I can see Troy turning pale...the security guard is pushing the packages out of the way. Troy's illegal activity, right there in the open for all to see. Fortunately for Troy, I am in too much pain right now to rat him out. And the security guard is much too busy with me to worry about why there are packages in the back of a dog catcher's van.

"Can you take the sweatpants off?" the security guard asks.

I shake my head. I don't think I could in a million years manage that sort of dexterity right now. Plus they're sticking to my legs, soaked with blood and God knows what else.

The security guard reaches into her pocket and pulls out a pair of scissors.

"What are you doing?" I ask as she inches closer to me.

"I'm going to cut them off so we can get you delivered." She cuts through my sweatpants (and my underwear, I think).

I lift my head to see that a crowd has formed behind the van, many faces peering into the back of the van. As Maria assured me earlier in my pregnancy, I don't even care right now.

The security guard recoils as she rips the remains of my sweatpants. "Holy smokes that's a head!"

"What?" I am sure I heard her wrong. "There's a head?"

"Yup and it's coming out right now," she says, slapping gloves on. "Don't push yet."

"I don't want to pu—"

She barely has time to put the gloves on before a monstrous pain washes over me and an overwhelming urge to push overtakes my body.

Crap. I'm going to give birth in the back of a dog catcher's van.

9.5

November

"Amy! Have you seen my tie?"

Roger dashes into the bedroom, face as red as a beet, sweat rolling down his cheeks. He is frantically attempting to pull his suit jacket on over his dress shirt, but his arm keeps getting stuck in the sleeve. It's pretty comically, actually. I try to stifle my laughter, but he sees me smirking.

"This isn't funny, Amy. It's my *first day* and I'm going to be late if I can't find my tie!"

"Do you really *need* a tie? I can hardly imagine that anyone would think less of you if you weren't wearing a tie today."

"Amy! I *need* a tie. Today is the day to make a good first impression. If I don't wear a tie today, none of them will take me seriously and I'll be the laughingstock of the place. At least for the next four years."

He looks at me, and for a second, I imagine him as a scared little boy leaving home without his mother for the very first time. I know that this day is important to him. He's been agonizing over it for weeks on end. Ever since he got the call—just after Allie was born. Like literally five minutes after she was born.

Robby Palmer, the guy they had hired for the principal position Roger had interviewed for eight months earlier, had up and quit. Well, apparently he had a nervous breakdown and needed to be carted off to the psychiatric ward, but the school board considered that "quitting" and asked Roger to step in effective November first.

Roger had been paralyzed by indecision. He wanted the job so badly, but he was nervous at the possibility that this job would result in him be carted off to the psych ward as well.

When I told him that I was out of a job myself—not only had I been fired, but I imagine that they frown upon their employees giving birth in the back of the dog catcher's van—he accepted the position. And now he looks like he's going to puke.

I take pity on him as I recall seeing a tie in the kitchen when I heated up Allie's bottle earlier.

"I think I saw a tie next to the microwave. Did you leave there by mistake?"

Roger's face lights up as he realizes, yes, he did leave the tie next to the microwave. He dashes out of the room and I chuckle to myself. My laughter startles the baby, who has fallen asleep, draped across my lap—the only way she *will* sleep.

Her eyes blink open and I cringe, anticipating the beginning of another one of her notorious screaming fits. She is only three weeks old and her hissy fits are already legendary. Much to my dismay, my mother is the only one who can get her to calm down once she starts, usually by patting her bottom in a specific way. And I don't want to have to call her today. I have had quite enough of my mother for the last three weeks. Dear God, if she drones on one more time about the scenario that led to Allie being born in the back of the animal control van—

But instead of screaming, Allie...*smiles*.

I gasp in shock, my hand on her bottom, ready to pat. *Is it a real smile?* Mom to 3 (er, Mom to 4) on the Baby Days forum said that babies only smile when they have gas when they're this little. *It probably is just gas.* My suspicions are confirmed by a rumbling of air escaping her back end.

Roger rushes back into the room, frantically wrapping his tie around his neck. He leans down to kiss me good-bye and pauses mid tie.

"Look at that, Amy! She's smiling at me!"

As if on cue, Allie's smile widens, making her father grin from ear to ear. I don't have the heart to tell him that it's just gas.

"Yup. She's wishing you luck today. Good luck. Knock 'em dead."

Roger is still beaming as he kisses the top of my head. "Well, as long as you two ladies are in my cheering squad, I'll always be a winner." He finishes tying the tie and waves to us before dashing out of the room.

As I roll my eyes at his cheesy sentiment, the cordless phone on the bed begins to ring. I squint, but I can't see the number on the caller ID from where I sit.

"Come on, kiddo." I lift Allie up and drape her across my shoulder. She's not a fan of that position and I am afraid she's going to start wailing as soon as I pick up the phone. I grimace as I press the talk button, but Allie seems relatively happy. Well, she's not screaming at least.

"Hello?" I cradle the phone between my ear and the shoulder that Allie is not leaning on.

There is a brief silence on the other end of the phone, but then I hear throat clearing.

"Amy?" A nasally voice meets my ears.

"Yes?" The voice sounds familiar, but I can't place it.

"This is Amanda? From ACC? The animal control center?"

Oh yes. *Amanda.*

I resist the urge to groan. *Why is the woman who was overjoyed when Bridget fired me calling? I got my last paycheck. There doesn't seem to be any other reason she would call.*

"Um, hi." I hope she gets to the point quickly so I can hang up and get on with my day. For the first time in three weeks I wish Allie would start wailing—at least I would have an excuse to get off the phone.

There's another break of silence followed by a deep sigh.

"Listen, Amy. The reason I'm calling...well, Bridget said to call actually—"

Gee, I thought Bridget liked me. Thanks Bridget. What'd I ever do to you?

"Bridget said to call because, well, Rodney's been arrested."

My heart stops in my chest. *Did she say* Rodney's *been arrested? What about Troy?*

After I had Allie in the van, Troy took off. I have no idea what happened to him or the packages. And honestly, I've been a little too busy and sleep deprived to look into it.

"Wait, what about Troy?"

More silence. I'm assuming now that the sound of silence is equivalent to the sound of Amanda eating some crow. I am imagining that Bridget is standing right in front of her so she can't say what she really thinks of me.

"Yes. Um, him too. It was because of the article in the paper."

Ah yes. The article by Julia Heart.

About the same time that Roger was being called to inform him of Allie's birth, I was being whisked away upstairs to the maternity floor—the floor I should have been on to give birth. You know, if I hadn't done so in the back of the animal control van and all that.

I was wheeled into my postpartum room and my jaw dropped. My roommate was none other than Julia Heart. Excuse me, Julia Heart Moore. She had gotten married last year, and had just had her first baby—a boy named Jasper.

Of course we got to talking and surprisingly, Julia remembered me, and only the good version of me from high school. She claimed that I had been one of the few people that had been nice to her back then.

Over the course of the next day, I discovered that Julia had never gotten my letter—she had been on maternity leave for the past six weeks—Jasper had been two weeks late. She was eager for details of what I had uncovered, and was scribbling away in her notepad as I told the story that culminated in giving birth in the back of animal control van. I asked her to leave that part out of the story—she did. The article was published last week.

Amanda's voice sounds small and meek, but she quickly covers up her half-hearted apology (if you can even call it that) by saying, "So you're unfired, I guess. Bridget wanted me to find out when you would be coming back to work."

Ah ha.

"So why didn't Bridget call me herself?"

I think I know the answer to this, but I have to be honest—if I'm enjoying Amanda squirming, Bridget is probably enjoying it as well.

"She said I needed to call. I'm the manager after all. She's right here."

Ah, so Bridget definitely wanted to see Amanda squirm.

"Well, I can't work right now. I have a three week old baby at home."

"Well not *now*, Amy. When you're ready to come back to work." Amanda manages to sound haughty, even though she's basically groveling to me, the person that she unceremoniously fired, hours before I gave birth.

"Who says I'd even want to come back to work, Amanda? You were pretty clear that I didn't belong there. Maybe I'm going to go work someplace else."

Throwing her own words in her face gives me a little thrill. This is the most fun I've had in three weeks. Also, I think I'm being a little bolder than I normally would be— being sleep deprived and all.

There is more silence, whispering, and then a *really* deep sigh. "Bridget said to tell you that there is a raise included. This is um, a salaried position.

Oh really?

I stare down at Allie as I hear Amanda breathing impatiently on the other end of the phone. The ball is truly in my court right now...for the first time in my life. Roger got his principal job, so I don't have to work right now if I don't want to. I can say yes and go back to the job I enjoyed, or I can say no, win this battle over Amanda, and get to do the job I *really* enjoy.

I glance down at my gurgling baby. And suddenly, this is a no-brainer.

"You know what, Amanda? I've got a better offer."

I hang up the phone and toss it on the bed.

Allie smiles at me again. Or has gas. Either way, it's sweet to see her toothless gums.

"You know what kid?" I tell her as I cradle her in my arms. "We're a pretty good team."

Heather Balog is a school nurse by day, supermom and writer by night. She lives near her beloved shore with her husband, children and one very needy dog, who thinks that he is human. When she is not writing, she's thinking about writing, reading, or tending to the needs one of the aforementioned people or pet. She also can be found cleaning things in the house that won't remain clean for longer than ten minutes, looking for missing socks, or running (away).

Other novels by Heather Balog:

Amy Maxwell & the 7 Deadly Sins

Amy Maxwell's 6th Sense

Amy Maxwell's 5th Child

The 4 Dilemmas of Amy Maxwell

The Quiet Boy

The Dead of Summer

Friends From the Edge

All She Ever Wanted

Letters to My Sister's Shrink

Note to Self: Change the Locks

When the Bough Breaks

Lexie Maxwell & One Spooky House

Lexie Maxwell & the Two New Kids

Best Friends & Other Liars

Sign up for my newsletter here

And get a FREE copy of Amy Maxwell & the 10 Days of Quarantine

Check out the blogs:

www.thebadmommydiaries.com

www.badmommyreads.com

Or Follow me: Facebook

Or Instagram